PROMISED TO A BOSS

TRENAE'

This book is dedicated to my heart and my headache, Ava Marie. There's no limit to what I would do to make sure there is always a smile on your face, gorgeous. Anything I do is for my light bright god-child. Nanny loves you and will move heaven and earth to make you smile.

To my sister, Asia Lewis. We the girls of the crew and swear we stay live! I can't thank you enough for giving me the opportunity to know and love Ava! Love ya gah.

To my brother, Kevin Lewis Jr. My giant I'm so proud of you for following your dreams and never giving up. You went to college and dominated the court as well as those classes and graduation is coming up. Love you my big lil brother.

ACKNOWLEDGMENTS

TWELFTH BOOK SHAWTTTTYYY!!!! LOL

This part never gets easy because of course I don't want to miss anyone. First and foremost, I want to thank God for giving me the gift of storytelling. I'm still shocked that I can actually create a story that you, my readers, love. It baffles me that I went through so much schooling just to end up coming back to what I've always loved, writing. I know that that was no one but God's doing. Without him there would be no Trenae' and for that I am forever grateful.

To my fiance' and best friend, Joe. You are the most supportive man a girl could ask for. You accept when I can't pay attention to you because I'm chasing the bag, you motivate me when I feel like giving up, you allow me to bounce ideas off of you and you even throw out titles. (Even if they suck and I never use them lol). I love you because even when I'm a mess, you love me. When I'm working on a book, I know I look a mess on the regular but you still tell me I'm the prettiest girl ever. I'm grateful for the times you start meals and clean the kitchen so that I can work. You are an amazing man and an amazing father. I love you forever and a day!

To my parents, Trudy, Keith and Tarunye thank you for the continued support. As soon as I say my book is live y'all quickly one-click and I definitely appreciate it.

To the women who played a huge role in raising me, my grandmother

Deloris, my aunt Betty and my aunt Mona, I appreciate every sacrifice you made to make sure I never went without anything I needed. Thank you for all that y'all do.

To my siblings, Kevin, Malika, Asia, Tarya, Makia, and Jayanma I love y'all and never forget that the sky is the limit.

To my Godchild and constant headache, Ava, anything that I do is for you! It's my job to make sure that smile never falls from your face and I'll work overtime to make sure that happens. Nanny loves you forever and a day Phat-Phat!

To my cousins that are more like siblings, Terrance (Keep ya head up cuz), Raquel, Reggie, Trevor and Boots I love y'all!

To my squuuuuaaaadddd lol, Chrissy, Fantasia and Kelleashia bruh so many of y'all stories find their way into my books. My characters are based off of y'all and everything, thanks for the constant laughs. Above all that thanks for remaining the same, y'all never switched up on the kid and I appreciate that. You know y'all stuck with me foreva (Cardi B voice).

Keondria, Secret, Kelleashia, Zatasha and Rikida, I can't thank y'all enough for the brutal honesty y'all give me. Y'all been rocking with me since The Sins of Beretta one and long after I have ended their story here you are all, still by my side. Y'all the best!

B Capri "Cardi B" Miller, my boo thang, you know there is nothing but love between us. In you I found not only a friend but a sister. And I got my brother AJ! LOL! You are such a beautiful person on the inside and that is complemented by your outer appearance. From the moment we spoke we just clicked! You motivate me to write when all I want to do is watch the firestick! When I have no more ideas to give, you throw random shit out. You stuck with me foreva!

Shakela James, if you aren't the face of strength then I don't know what is. Time after time I have watched this industry attempt to break you and here you still stand, unbreakable. Your determination, resilience and will power to keep excelling in this industry despite it all is admirable, to say the least. Meeting you in person was a breath of fresh air. You are so genuine and unapologetically YOU! I pray for your peace of mind and your well-being, daily!

Coco Shawnde, my black barbie and one of my best friends. You are one of the most hard working woman that I personally know. There isn't a day that goes by that you don't inspire me. You've went from being someone that I spoke with from time to time to being family. I love how caring, goofy and motivating you are. Plus, you love Gates so you gotta be lit. I pray that your season for winning in this industry is near! You are dope and baby they have to stop sleeping on you soon.

Ebonee Abby, my friend and mentor. I am so appreciative to have someone like you in my life. In a world full of takers, you are a giver of many things. I come to you for so many things, I should cut you a damn check. You never turn me away and I always end up with way more information than I bargained for. Thank you a million times!

Monique, you push me when I don't want to be pushed. You push me when I don't know I NEED to be pushed. Yo push me when I'm already pushing myself. Your motivation and reminders to secure the bag is everything. Thanks for being you!

Zatasha, the book plug herself! What you do for me and countless other authors is remarkable. You bridge the gap from author to reader and I appreciate you because of it. You are an amazing woman and I speak for many authors and readers when I say we are forever thankful for what you do! I love youuuuuu Z!!!

To my sisters in pen and my bad and boujie clique, Demetrea, Jas, Tina, T'anne Marie, Sunni, Coco, B Capri and my boo thang Lanae (whew)! You are an amazing set of women who help this word count challenges and long days fly by. The endless jokes and countless heart to hearts are always the best. You all motivate me in your own ways and I am glad that we had the opportunity to form this bond. Love you all!

To my publisher, the creator of my baby King, the literary grim reaper and the banger dropper herself, Mz Lady P!!! I can't thank you enough honey. You took a chance on me and I appreciate that forever. As I'm learning you as a publisher and a friend your hustle rubs off on me. You push me more than I have ever been pushed in my life. You inspire me more than you know!

To my sisters of KBC thanks for y'all continued support, Love y'all.

Last but most certainly not least, to YOU my readers, I cannot thank you *all enough for continuing to rock with me. Y'all took a chance on a new author and been rocking with me since! I will strive to never let y'all down. Thanks for the inboxes and reviews on my past work, I definitely took everything y'all said into consideration. I have to also thank y'all for being patient with me, as I got this book done for you all.*

If I missed anyone, know that it wasn't intentional. Charge my memory and not my heart for that mistake.

I hope you enjoy my new series because these characters took me for a ride and never stopped talking to me!

WANT TO KEEP UP WITH TRENAE'?

FACEBOOK: PAREE TRENAE

Facebook: Author Trenae'
Instagram: Trenaedhaplug
Twitter: Ooh_Paree_Dear
Snapchat: Paree Trenae
Periscope: Paree Trenae
Add my reader's group: Trenae' Presents: The Juice

SYNOPSIS

Synopsis

Tired, fed up, and overworked were just a few of the words that could be used to describe Kewyn (key wine) Daniels. She was the victim of being in a relationship out of guilt rather than out of love. As average as her feelings about her love life may have been, her relationship was as far from the word average as possible. Though Ty had Kewyn's heart because of the past the two shared, it wasn't enough to make her walk away from the chemistry she and Dez shared. Instead of choosing between the two, she decided to offer Ty what men dreamed of. A relationship with both women. What worked for a while had Kewyn feeling like the relationship is cluttered, but her breath of fresh air was on the way.

Adonis Parker didn't intend to fall for the chocolate bombshell, but surprisingly he couldn't control this. Sometimes the universe brought some sunshine into your night and there was nothing you could do to block it out. Though his friends and family see a change in him, something is stopping him from fully committing to Kewyn and the secret she is keeping is enough to knock down everything they've built.

Shailen or Shay as she is affectionately known as, is all about breaking the rules. Not even being the sister of one of the most feared me in the city could stop Shay from doing whatever she wanted. Including running off to get married behind his back. The problem now, she is bored in her marriage and an old flame has returned causing her to want that old thing back. What happens when that old thing comes with baggage of his own tough?

Corey "Corrupt" Matthews, has returned back home and back to his position as Adonis' right hand man. Though he loves his girl-friend Mika, sometimes love just ain't enough. Especially when its now battling with feelings he has always felt for his best friend's baby sister. Things have changed, and they are both ready to take what they had to the next level, but love is never an easy game when there are too many players on the field. In this explosive tale of love, lies and secrets everyone can't live happily ever after when skeletons won't stay in the closet. Old bonds will break, and new bonds will be built but can bonds built on a lie last when the past won't stay where it was left?

1

Kewyn

"Ok, that's a wrap for me, this was my last room." I happily called out to my coworker. After working twelve hours cleaning rooms, my feet and back were killing me and I wanted nothing more than to soak in a hot bubble bath. Alone.

"I have two left man." Lanae said with a frown on her beautiful face. I wanted to ignore her ass as she filled her cart but I fucked with her the long way, so I knew I wouldn't. Rolling my eyes toward God, I released a sigh before a smile filled her face.

"Don't smile at me hoe. What's the damn room number you want me to take?" I asked throwing my wallet and keys back in my locker and making sure it was secure. Though the hotel was nice, these hoes would steal communion from the church if the opportunity presented itself. I spun around just as Lanae made her way over to me and pulled me in a bear hug.

"Thank you so much Cakes, you know I'm tired as fuck. Good looking out." She said calling me by the nickname she gave me when I first started working here. She said I had more cake than Betty Crocker and Lil Debbie combined so the name Cakes, was born.

Before I could reply to her, I felt her hands slip to my ass and quickly pulled away.

"Don't play with me Lanae." I snapped.

"What's the big deal? It ain't like you don't go that way." She said shrugging.

"What's the room number?" I asked while rolling my eyes. Her ass knew how to get under my skin. Though we were as tight as I would ever get with a coworker, I regret confiding in her the dynamics of my relationship. From the moment I had opened my fat ass mouth, she felt like she could take my girlfriend, Dez's place. Even after I told her ass there was no opening for that position, she would still shoot her shot like her name was Kobe.

"Don't be like that Cakes, you know I love you bitch. Anyway, take the presidential suite. It's the easiest room because dude is some type of neat freak and he is never there." She said making me side eye her ass.

"Last time you recommended that I take a certain room, I walked in on a motherfucking orgy!" I spat as she fell out laughing.

"Man no, it is not like that I swear." She paused as she continued to laugh. "His suite really is the easiest to clean. His ass folds his dirty towels and leaves them in a neat stack right outside of the bathroom door. For the most part he cleans up behind himself, plus that man so fucking fine you need to see him. Every woman needs to lay eyes on a God like him at least once." She said fanning herself. "Girl thinking of his ass done got me all wet between the thighs." She said, and I used that as my cue to get the hell out of there. After double checking my cart to make sure it was fully stocked, I made my way to the elevators where I was met by a nigga so fine he had to be a figment of my imagination. He was in a deep conversation on his cell phone, but his eyes stared into mine like I had his undivided attention. I wasn't even aware that I had stopped walking until the damn doors closed on my face.

"God damn!" I said aloud.

"Why are you looking at the elevator like that?" Lanae asked walking up behind me. I shook my head at her ass because Lanae did whatever the fuck she wanted to over here. We were supposed to be dressed in these ugly ass black dresses with the hotels logo on it that was made from the same material as scrubs, with a pair of black stocking, black shoes and a white apron. Her ass chose to wear a pair of black tights that had her huge ass and pussy print front and center, she had on a company t-shirt that made for the maintenance people and a pair of black air max. I don't understand why her ass was never told anything, no warnings, write ups or anything. "You see something you like?" she asked catching me looking her over.

"Bitch, you wish." I snapped while playfully rolling my eyes. The truth was, Lanae was bad as fuck. She was drop dead gorgeous and had a body that people would kill for. Lil mama was stacked, and she knew it and flaunted that shit.

"I do wish. I wish you would give me one hour and I would have your ass begging me to replace that other bitch. She ain't even cute." She said throwing her hands on her full lips. Hitting the up arrow on the elevator, I ignored her ass. "Ok, play with it if you want to." She said walking away. Once the elevator opened, I walked in and pressed the P2 button for the penthouse. I had to slide in my master key card because the elevator would have denied me access if I hadn't. I felt my apple watch vibrating and saw that I had a text from Ty. I didn't even read it because I knew it would aggravate my soul. I would read that once I finished this last room. When the doors opened, I pushed my cart off of the elevator and into the little area between the elevator doors and the double doors of the suite. Knocking on the door, I waited a few seconds before knocking again. When I didn't hear anything, I slid my key in the door and opened it.

"Housekeeping!" I called out but was met with silence. Rolling my cart further in, I grabbed my gloves and a trash bag so that I could gather all the trash from the cans around the room. Lanae wasn't lying, his room was really neat. Stripping the bed, I threw his bedding into the hamper attached to my basket and grabbed a new set. It took no time for me to disinfect the bed and perfectly remake it. I know for a fact that some of the staff would remake the bed with exact same bedding and that was disgusting to me. It wasn't like they were running up their own water bill when we did laundry so just swap the shit out. Before vacuuming, I always sprayed my bathrooms so that the cleaner could sit for a while, so I grabbed the Clorox bathroom cleaner and went to do that. I went to open the bathroom door, but the door knob turned before I could even touch it. "Fuck!" I said dropping my bottle and the towels I was holding and grabbing my chest. I couldn't even catch my breath because as soon as I was over the shock he took my breath away again. This man was as naked as the day he came into this world and my God, he was blessed.

"The fuck you doing in my room?" He asked. It was the same man from the elevator but just that fast he pissed me off with his rude ass.

"Well, as you can see from my uniform I work here. And I definitely knocked and announced my presence twice!" I snapped back. His ass didn't even react from my lil attitude. In fact, he rubbed his chin hair and laughed at my ass.

"Your ass was supposed to clean my room since earlier any fucking way, you a lil late and I called for towels since this morning. I assume you got some and yo ass better not try to hand me those dirty bitches you just dropped on the floor." He said pushing past me. He slid me to the side by grabbing my waist and I damn near stopped breathing when his dick rubbed against my thigh.

"First of all, this ain't my damn room to clean. I was doing someone a favor by helping her out!" I said going to the cart and grabbing a few more towels. I threw him a body towel and went to the restroom with the rest. I noticed from the steam that he had just took a shower so that's why he didn't hear me. Rolling my eyes in frustration, I sprayed the bathroom down and chose to stay in here cleaning. Hopefully, once I was done he would be gone so I could finish the rest of the suite in peace. As I scrubbed everything from the sink to the toilet and shower down, I kept thinking about that damn midget leg he had for a dick. I had only been with one man in my life and I thought his dick was big, so I knew I wouldn't know what to do with all of that dick he was carrying around. Finishing with the bathroom, I dragged my feet back into the room and this nigga was dead ass laying on top of the covers still butt ass naked. I shook my head as I went about cleaning the room like he wasn't there. I felt his eyes on me, but I didn't say a word and neither did he. His black ass was weird as fuck and I was happy to be done. Normally, I would have told him have a good day before leaving but fuck him. I pushed my cart out and before the door closed I could have sworn I heard his ass laughing.

"Bitch, did you see his fine ass?" Lanae asked as soon as I walked back into the supply room.

"The better question is, why the fuck it looks like your ass been sitting in here? Did you go clean a room while I was helping your ass out?" I asked with my hands on my hips.

"Calm down cakes, I swear I just finished mine like five minutes ago, I was waiting on you. You need a ride?" She asked, and I knew she was lying because she didn't make eye contact with me. I was hella good at reading people and I could tell she was on some bull-shit, I would never help her again.

"Yeah ok, see if I don't leave your ass by yourself next time. I drove myself here today so I'm cool." I said leaving the cart and grabbing my things.

"What time you work tomorrow?" She asked.

"I don't, I took my vacation so see you in a couple weeks." I said before walking out. I wasn't even happy about taking vacation because truth be told, I didn't want to be at my own damn house. I would actually rather be at work than to deal with what I had going on at home. Hopping in my brand new Nissan Altima, I inhaled the new car scent. I had been working overtime to get my baby and I was proud of myself when I got her. I opened the sunroof as Yo Gotti's I Am album blasted through my speakers. This was my shit and would forever be in rotation. I decided to make a few stops before going home, I knew I was just prolonging my alone time.

"WHERE YOU BEEN?" My boyfriend Ty asked before I could even step over the door step properly.

"Hey Ty, my day went well and yours?" I asked rolling my eyes at his ass. Lately, I had been feeling like this wasn't what I wanted anymore. I knew I deserved more than I was getting but I also knew that it was damn near my own fault, so I took it.

"Hey Key, how was work?" Dez asked walking over and kissing my lips. What I thought would be a quick peck, turned into so much more when she slid her tongue in my mouth. Even when she knew I wasn´t in the mood, Dez always went for what he wanted. That's what attracted me to her, she was so bold and in your face. After biting down on my lip, she let me go. "I ran you some bath water earlier, but I'll have to warm it up, meet me upstairs and I'll take your mind off of whatever pissed you off." She said, walking away and twisting out the room. I watched her fat ass shake in the lace boy shorts she wore and smirked. Dez was my girlfriend and as I stated, Ty was my man. Our relationship was far from regular, but it worked for a few years, Though Ty loved the perks of dating two women, it wasn't his idea. This was all the results of me falling in love with two people.

"Can you grab these bags?" I asked rolling my eyes at Ty. Reluctantly, he threw the remote controller down and came grab the bags that I had carried in. When he reached for a kiss, I turned my head on his ass and he caught my cheek.

"Dez can get a kiss but I can't?" He asked.

"Dez didn't try to kiss my mouth with hers smelling like a damn pack of Kools." I responded before walking past him. Making it to the only bedroom in the apartment, I sat on the bed and started taking my clothes off. I noticed the panties and bra that Dez had on were on the floor, so I knew she was already in the tub waiting on me.

"Can I use your car real quick?" Ty asked, throwing the bags on the bed.

"No, you can take the other one like you normally do!" I replied.

"Man, I want to ride in the new one! The fuck is your problem Kewyn? You only been here but a few seconds and you have an attitude!" He screamed.

"She only been here but a few seconds and you already asking her for some shit. Damn, let her unwind!" Dez spat swinging the bathroom door open. I appreciated her for standing up for me, but this was one of my main problems. This fucking relationship was too crowded.

"Mind your fucking business Dez! I'm talking to Kewyn not yo dumb ass!" He snapped on her.

"I wasn't dumb a second ago nigga." She said letting me know they had just fucked. I didn't care about that too much because we all fucked whether it was all three parties or just two.

"Here Ty, don't fucking smoke in my car and don't ride your lil friends in my shit." I said throwing him the keys. His ass didn't say anything, he just ran out of there. I didn't even care, and I just wanted him gone. Over the past few months, I realized that I didn't like the person that he was becoming. His drive was gone, and he was turning me off. I loved the hell out of Ty because he was the only constant thing in my life when I didn't know where it was going. We had known each other since we were kids but as I grew up, he didn't. I wanted more than to be the woman of some corner boy and he couldn't grasp that fact. I think we were only together at this point because Dez was the tape holding us together. When she and I met, Ty was in jail and I had needs. He told me I couldn't fuck with another nigga because he was the only dick that touched my pussy and he wanted to keep it that way. What he didn't predict, and I didn't expect was for me to fall for a woman. Dez and I actually met, while leaving visitation. I was waiting on the bus and she was passing in her car. This wasn't the first time we had seen each other but we never spoke to one another until that day. She offered me a ride home, and I accepted because I was tired as hell. After that two hour drive, she had me considering being with a woman for the first time in my life. Then we started kicking it and taking that weekly ride together. The dynamics changed on the visitation when her dude broke up with her. She was crying, and I was being a friend and consoling her. We decided to stay in town rather than take the two hour drive and had dinner and drinks. After one too many drinks, we got a room and she ended up having my pussy as desert. This went on for two years and then Ty told me he had a month before he was released. I tried to leave her alone but we both found ourselves sick because we had fallen in love. I knew I didn't want to be without her, but Ty wouldn't live without me. So, I laid everything on the table for him and basically told him that I was still going to see her. He thought it was a joke and didn't take me serious until his ass walked into my apartment and she had moved in. He felt some type of way until he found out that we would all benefit from this sexually. What man wouldn't accept that offer?

"Let me make you feel better." Dez said undressing me. She kissed the top of my pussy as she pulled my thong and stockings down and I couldn't help but to moan out. When she grabbed my hand, I followed her into the bathroom where we sank into the bubbles. "Come here." She said pulling me on her lap and bringing my lips down to hers. I hungrily returned her kiss as her fingers toyed at the lips of my pussy.

"Fuck Dez." I moaned into her mouth.

"Don't worry about Ty. You know he loves you and its going get better once he gets this plug. Ok?" She asked, and I refused to answer her. "Key, you head me?" She asked. "Oh alright." Without another word, she reached in the tub and it wasn't long before I knew what she was reaching for. My eyes crossed as she shoved a toy into my pussy before turning the jack rabbit on. Even though the toy was pushing in and out of me on its own, that didn't stop her from pulling it out and slamming it back inside of me.

"OH MY FUCKING GOD!" I screamed.

"I said its going get better!" She repeated. "You not goin leave us. Right?" She asked driving the toy deeper into my pussy.

"Right baby, right! I'm never going to leave ya'll!" I screamed out my answer while bouncing on the toys and nutting. Between my love for them and the fact that they both made me submit with sex, I wasn't sure I would ever leave.

2

T^y Jamming Meek Mill's song, I'm A Boss, I felt like just that as I pulled up to Turning Heads hair salon and parked. I pulled out my phone and sent a text before lighting up a blunt filled with some bomb ass weed. Putting my head back on the headrest, I thought about the moves I was about to make in the game. For years, I tried to fight my way to the top and with little to no effort, Dez put me in position to do just that. Lately I found myself wanting to be around Dez more than I wanted to be around Kewyn and that shit was crazy because I always thought Kewyn would be the only woman I loved. The more time Kewyn spent away from home, the happier I seemed to be. Her ass was always complaining about some shit and shooting down my ideas while Dez was the complete opposite. Dez would roll me up a blunt and listen to my ideas all while sucking my dick. She was supposedly in this shit for Kewyn but seemed to be sliding down my dick more and more lately. I peeped how her ass would talk Kewyn into taking more hours at work just so we could be alone. If she knew like I knew, she would peep how it would never be just her and I. I was on some other shit.

"Wassup baby!" Lisha said sliding in the passenger seat and

reaching over for a kiss. "How long do I have you for today? I cleared my schedule for the next couple hours." She said, leaning her seat back and putting her feet on the dash board.

"Shit, the next couple hours then. What you want for lunch?" I asked looking at her thick ass thighs that were exposed in the small ass skirt she was rocking. "Why you wore that short shit to work knowing all those fucking barbers be in your face? Get fucked up Felisha!" I warned calling her by her full name.

"Now, you know I don't want nobody but you! Fuck them niggas, they can't do nothing for me!" She said rubbing my dick through my basketball shorts I wore. "Take the left here." She said directing me through traffic. I followed her directions thinking she was leading me to wherever she wanted her food from but instead we pulled up to an abandoned building.

"Man, what the fuck you on?" I asked.

"I can order some food when I get back to work, I want some dick and I want it now. Pull up behind the building and let your seat back." She said already removing her thongs and throwing them on the floor. I sped behind the building and put the car in park with my dick standing at attention. Lifting my ass from the seat, I pulled my basketball shorts and boxers down and pushed the seat back as far as it would go. Hopping up on her knees, she bent over and licked the tip of my dick before moaning like that shit was dipped in chocolate. I wonder if she was tasting the flavor of Dez's pussy on my shit cause right before Kewyn came home I was damn near standing in Dez pussy. Just thinking of how Dez was throwing it back on a nigga made me grab Lisha by the hair and fuck her throat. She made noise like she couldn't handle it but quickly recovered and started handling the dick like I knew she could. I was fucking her mouth, but visions of Dez squirting on my dick had me ready to bust.

"Watch out ma, I ain't ready to bust. I want that pussy." Grabbing her hand, I pulled her on to my lap and pulled her skirt over her ass, so it was bundled at her waist before plunging my dick into her wet pussy. That shit was gripping my dick so tight that I could barely move in the mother fucker. "God damn! This pussy got my dick in a death grip!" I said grabbing her ass with both hands and grinding her pussy into my dick. Her mouth was set in a silent o and I knew she couldn't make a sound if she wanted to. Fuck the cat having her tongue, this dick had her tongue. After getting her adjusted to my size, I put my hands behind my head and got in a relaxed position.

"What you doing? Why you stopped?" She asked, looking at me like I was crazy.

"Shit, cause I'm about to hit this gas and let you handle the dick." I said grabbing the prerolled blunt and lighting it.

"I got ya!" She said sitting back. Her ass was so fat she sat on the wheel and blew the damn horn. "My bad." She laughed while taking off her bra and t-shirt and throwing it on the passenger side of the car. She hit a button on side of the seat that lifted the bottom part of it and made me sit up higher. With one foot on the arm of the door and the other on the arm rest, she started bouncing up and down on my dick. I took a big ass puff of the blunt I was smoking and held it in for a second while watching her juices wet my dick. Hands down, Felisha had the best pussy I had ever been in. This shit was always virgin tight and wet like a lake. Another thing about it is I knew no one else had been in this bitch and never would. Like I did with Kewyn, I broke her in, but the difference was that she never fucked another nigga or bitch. Kewyn ass couldn't wait for a nigga, she proved that she wasn't loyal, so I treated that shit with disloyalty of my own. Taking another hit of the blunt, I blew it in Lisha's face. Without fucking up her rhythm, she grabbed the blunt and hit it. With my mouth free, I popped one of her titties in my mouth and sucked on her nipple.

"Fuck this dick Felisha! Kewyn was fucking me better than this, I could have stayed home for all that!" I lied, smacking her ass and gripping her cheeks. I knew I said the magic phrase because her ass started riding the fuck out of my dick. She didn't even know Kewyn, but she hated her ass cause she had me. "Fuck man, my dick head so sensitive. Quit grinding against my dick!" I roared feeling my nut rising. I quickly lifted her up cause I wasn't ready just yet. "Get out!" I demanded. She got out the car and I reached in the back for the blanket that Kewyn kept in her back seat. She would have her lunch breaks in her car and fall asleep with it. I placed the blanket on the hood of the car and lifted Lisha so that she was laying on top of it. Putting her legs on my shoulders, I shoved my dick back into her pussy and went to work.

"Ohhhhhhhmy gooosssshhhhhhhh! Wait Ty, wait!" She said trying to slow me down with her hand

"Move that fucking hand and fuck this dick back Lisha! I'll pull my dick out and go let Kewyn or Dez handle me!" I teased and just like I knew she would, she moved her hand and started grinding back on my dick. Moments later, I shot my seeds deep in her pussy. I took a step back and beat my dick against her pussy as a few more shots of nut shot out on her lower stomach.

"Damn that was good!" She said jumping up and going into the car and returning with wipes. She cleaned my dick off before getting herself together.

"You spoke to your brother lately?" I asked.

"I knew that was the only reason you came scoop me up Tyreek." She replied rolling her eyes and turning her back on me. She bent down and wiped her pussy but the way her ass spread, woke my dick up again. Walking over to her, I grabbed her around the waist and rubbed my finger along her pussy lips. I felt her shudder in my arms and knew I was about to hit this shit again. Hell, she knew I had a healthy ass sexual appetite.

"Chill out, you know I came scoop you up because I missed your ass. I damn sure missed this gushy shit!" I said grabbing her pussy with my hand before sliding two fingers in her and easing them in and out.

"I- I fe-feel like you using me- me!" She tried to focus on her sentence.

"How am I using you ma. You approached me, you wanted this dick and I gave it to you. Remember what you told me?" I asked speeding up my fingers. "You said you wanted me to fuck you since we were younger! I told you what you had to do for me and you agreed." I said before removing my fingers and plunging my dick back into her!

"Oh My God!" She screamed out.

"Nah, don't call God. Tell me what I want to hear before I walk the fuck away from what we got." I lied. I had fallen for her young ass and I couldn't stay away if I wanted to. Though the information she gave me was important if I was going to take over, it wasn't the only reason I couldn't stay away. She was in love with me too and was willing to take anything I gave her in return for the information that she gave. I fucked her damn lace front crooked and as she lay over the hood of the car catching her breath, she told me all her brother's personal business. Chris Brown wasn't playing when he said these hoes wasn't loyal.

3

K ewyn
"Good morning beautiful." Ty said, walking over and kissing my lips. I returned his kiss appreciating the taste of the spearmint flavored mouth wash he used after brushing his teeth.

"You're in a good mood." I said smiling and fixing him a plate of pancakes, sausage, eggs and grits and placing it in front of him.

"Can't blame a nigga after last night, with yo nasty ass." He replied, causing me to laugh. Last night was the first time in a long time that the three of us had an amazing sex session. I woke up from a dead sleep with my pussy in Dez's mouth and Ty standing off to the side beating his dick. He wasn't there for long because as soon as Dez got "his pussy ready for him", like he instructed her to, he was plunging into my pussy and driving me crazy.

"I was the innocent one out of the equation, I was sleeping when you two freaks woke me up." I said, with my hands up. "Is Dez still sleeping?" I asked.

"Yeah, you know she's not a morning person. What time you work today?"

"Umm, eleven." I lied. I was forced to take my two weeks of paid vacation or they would be taken from me but that didn't mean I was just sitting in the house. I need some me time and I was taking it today. I had plans of going to the movies, lunch and then the spa and no one was changing those plans.

"You know it already ten, right? You should hurry up and go change, why did you put on those clothes anyway." Ty said looking at his phone. I felt like he was rushing me and that was strange because he always complained about all the hours I worked.

"Yeah, I'm sitting in at the front desk today, so I don't have to wear my uniform. I'll just throw a blazer over this." I said referring to the fitted light wash blue jeans, white silk shirt and camel colored heels I wore. My hair was cut in a bob and layered to perfection.

"Oh Ok, that's Wassup. You look cute." He complimented me, and we fell into a peaceful conversation as we finished breakfast. My movie was starting in another thirty minutes, so I excused myself and went up the stairs. Dez was still snoring but that didn't stop me from climbing in between her legs and kissing all over her face.

"I got some other lips for you to kiss too." She laughed as I got up from the bed. "What time you get off?" She asked, checking her watch for the time.

"Around four." I lied with ease. "You have clients today?" I asked.

"Nope. I'm just going to hang with Ty until you come back." She said rolling her eyes.

"Play nice, I love you." I said before leaving the house and speeding to the theatre. It felt so good to sit back and enjoy the damn near empty theatre and I almost was going to sit for another movie, but my stomach growling made me change my mind. I drove around town trying to decide what I wanted to eat and then the lobster mac and cheese from Ruth Chris crossed my mind and helped me make my mind up. Handing my keys to the valet driver, I entered the restaurant and wanted to cry because it was so packed.

"Welcome to Ruth Chris, are you meeting someone?" The host asked.

"No, just me." I responded.

"Ok, would you like a table or booth?" she asked again looking at the seating chart.

"Table please."

"Ok, right this way please." She said leading me to a table that appeared to be in the very middle of the restaurant. Looking towards the back of the restaurant, I had to do a double take before I chucked it up to me tripping.

"Hey, hey. I'm Sarah and I'll be your waitress today. Here is your menu. Can I get you started with a drink?" She asked.

"Yep. I'll take a long island tea." I said knowing that I was a light-weight when it came to my liquor.

"I'll be right back with that for you." She replied walking away. Looking at the menu, I felt someone looking at me and I quickly looked around the restaurant. I didn't see anyone obviously looking at me, so I shrugged it off and focused on the menu once again. "Here we are." The waitress said placing my drink down. "Can I get you started with an appetizer?" She asked but before I could answer, I was interrupted.

"Kewyn, this doesn't look like work." Dez said looking at me with a smirk.

"Yeah, they didn't need me, so I came to get a bite to eat. I thought I saw Ty walking into the restroom." I said, nodding as the waitress aid she would be back.

"Look, get up and walk to the restroom with me real quick." She said confusing me. Placing a napkin over my drink, I followed her. Before she walked into the women's bathroom, she looked around and went into the men's bathroom instead, dragging me with her. Ty was standing against the wall but when he saw me his eyes opened wide.

"The fuck she doing here? This why you told me to come to the bathroom and wait? Nigga we supposed to be handling business." He spazzed.

"What fucking business y'all was handling that I had to be excluded from? Huh? Y'all keeping secrets and shit?" I asked.

"Man chill out! We trying to make some moves, so your ass can stop tripping about how much money I'm not bringing in!" Ty spat.

"Aye, we can sit here and go back and forth until we blue in the fucking face or we can make this money." Dez said interrupting what was sure to be an argument. "Now look, Don ready to walk away because he doesn't trust your ass Ty! You out here acting like you don't need him when the truth is you do." She said.

"Then why the fuck you brought me to this bitch? You made it seem like the nigga was already on board!" Ty spat as someone attempted to push open the locked bathroom door. After another push, they walked away.

"Look, Kewyn I need you to do a favor for us. It's not that big of a deal and when its all said and done, you can quit that damn hotel and I don't have to cut another fucking head." Dez explained.

"I like my job." I said, with a shrug. "So, y'all can handle this shit on y'all own like y'all been doing in private." Cause fuck them, don't include me in shit now. I turned to walk away but Dez grabbed me.

"Chill man, we need you. Don been staring at you since you walked in, and he seems interested in you. I kind of lied and told him you were Ty's sister and I could set y'all up on a date." I wanted to slap the fuck out of Dez for even saying that dumb shit to me.

"What the fuck you mean on a date, bitch is you stupid?" Ty asked. It felt good to see that type of reaction from him.

"The nigga don't trust you so I told him if you could trust him with your sister then he could trust us with his product. It's a fucking date, nothing more and nothing less. He ain't even want to do it, I had to talk him into it. The nigga said y'all met before anyway!" She said, shocking me and Ty.

"Where the fuck yo sneaky pussy ass met this nigga at?" Ty asked, grabbing my arm.

"Ty let me go, I don't fucking know nobody named Don. I go to work and back the fuck home so how did I meet anyone? He must have the wrong fucking person!" I snapped.

"Nah, he studied the fuck out of you. Even said where you work." I mugged Dez when she said that shit.

"Dez, why you starting shit? I don't know that nigga!" I spat.

"Look, since you already acquainted, you may as well go entertain the nigga!" Ty spat.

"Really? You really cool with my going on a date with some random ass nigga? You too Dez? Like y'all cool using me as a damn bargaining tool?" My damn feelings were crushed and there was no way around that. I noticed Dez looked ashamed of herself but Ty looked unbothered.

"Maybe we can handle this a different way. My bad Key, I was focused on the money and I wasn't thinking clear." Dez apologized, but Ty stood there stone faced.

"Ty, you don't care?" I needed to know how he felt. When he looked me in my eyes and slightly shrugged his shoulders, tears of anger and hurt fell from my eyes. "That's a bet. I swear to God I hope that nigga is the perfect gentleman on this date. I hope he wines and dines me and shows me that he's a real man! Cause if he is, I'm goin be the perfect hoe! I'm going fuck that nigga so good he gives y'all the keys to his fucking empire just to keep me!" I spat, mugging them both.

"Don't fucking play with me Kewyn!" Ty barked walking closer to me.

"Whose playing?" I asked looking around. "Want to treat me like Pretty Woman, huh? Put me in the arms of a made nigga and shit, well I'm about to let his ass clean up! Remember how pretty woman ended nigga, just remember. Where the fuck he at?" I asked mugging Dez. Her ass hesitated a second too long because I stormed out in search of a nigga that looked boss like, whatever that meant. I knew they couldn't be sitting where I was because I would have noticed them. Walking to the other side, my eyes fell on the guy from the hotel and I swear my breath got shallow. This couldn't be my fucking life. I noticed he had two other chairs at the table with him with untouched food, so I knew he was the right person. I quickly wiped at the tears that pooled my eyes and walked over to him. He was on a phone call and his rude ass didn't hang up when I took a seat next time him. Instead, he continued talking but his eyes stare into mine.

"Corrupt, let me handle this situation. I'll be heading home shortly." He said, I know damn well this nigga didn't call me a situation. "Why every time I see you, you look like you're mad at the world?" He asked, as Ty and Dez walked back hand in hand. My stomach turned because I realized in that moment how close they had become. Was I now the outsider in my relationship? Did I really even care?

"This is your second time seeing me so what do you mean, every time?" I questioned, lifting my perfectly arched eyebrow.

"The time when you were staring at my dick was your first time seeing me, not my first time seeing you." He said before looking at Ty. "Something wrong? I see you balled up your fist." He asked, damn nearing hoeing Ty.

"Nah, I'm cool." Ty said with his face frowned up. I didn't even attempt to contain the laugh that erupted from my throat.

"Damn bro, he pulled your hoe card." I said laughing and shaking my head. Fuck Ty and Dez for this shit. "So," I said looking at Don. "I hear we have plans." I said smirking.

"Your mean ass cool with that?" He asked. "It wasn't my idea but I'm not going turn down the chance to spend some one on one time with you."

"Yeah, I'm good with it. After dealing with a fuck boy that didn't know how to stick up for me, I just hope you're more of a man than he was. Hell, nobody can be any worse than the situation I just got out of." I said, throwing hella shade. Dez and Ty had mugs on their faces but that was their problems. You know the phrase, hurt people hurt people. Don just chuckled as he paid the bill that was left on the table. I hadn't even eaten anything, but my appetite was long gone.

"Ty, Dez nice doing business with y'all. Corrupt will be in touch about that other thing." He responded standing to his feet. When he walked over and pulled my chair out, I was stunned for a second. Ty never did this shit. I placed my hand in his outstretched one and with his help I stood up and walked out without a second glance at Ty and Dez. I noticed that Don was leading me to his G wagon and I pulled back. "You good?" He asked. I looked back at my car and I noticed that Ty was attempting to storm our way but Dez was holding him back.

"Let me give them my keys." I said. I really just wanted to leave them with something to think about. Making my way over it looked like Ty wanted to apologize or at the very least change his mind, I wasn't going to give him a chance to though. "One more thing, don't think I didn't notice that you too got real fucking close behind my back. I just don't give a fuck. If we are being completely honest, I've outgrown this shit ages ago. I been wanting to say something, but I cared about y'all feelings too much. This right here though, I don't know if we can come back from this shit. Don't wait up for me tonight." I called after throwing the keys towards Dez and damn near jogging away. I didn't know what this night held for me, but I knew that on tomorrow, I had a decision to make. I knew that I loved Ty at one point because he loved me when no one else did. I also knew that I loved Dez because she loved me differently than anyone else did. But, I also knew that I loved myself more because no one would love me better than I would!

4

Adonis

I knew something wasn't right in this lil meeting we had just had but I was too blinded by this lil obsession I had with a woman I didn't even know. Of course, the physical is what made me take a second glance in her direction. She was around 5'7 and had skin the color of brown sugar. I loved the glow her skin had, like she was carrying the sun deep inside of her. I kept stealing glances at her body cause that shit was sick. It was damn near perfect, from her perky breast to her flat stomach, on down to her wide hips and that fat ass. I was definitely an ass man, so I was in love with the fact that she had way more ass than she knew what to do with it. I could tell from the way it jiggled despite the tightness of her jeans that this was God given and not man made. Just looking at the way her hips spread in the seats of my truck had me wondering why someone hadn't popped a few babies in her. These were definitely baby making hips.

"You have kids?" I asked.

"No. You?" She shot back. I simply shook my head no. I didn't know why I even asked her that shit. I knew that despite how this time together went, this couldn't be long term. In my line of work, it was rare that I even entertained a woman for anything other than a quick nut, but I felt myself hoping this could be more. "Where are we going?" She asked looking out the window.

"New Orleans, we can shop for you some clothes once we make it to my house." I answered. She didn't seem to care as she offered a shrug and glanced at her phone. That shit was going off alerting her of a multiple text messages and after a while she just powered her phone off. I wanted to ask her if it was a nigga calling, but that wasn't my place. At least not yet.

"Can I put something on the radio?" She asked. I handed her my iPhone since it was hooked up to the Bluetooth system. She browsed through the songs I had already downloaded, and I guess she didn't see what she wanted because she went to the search option and started typing. After a few seconds Lauryn Hill blasted through the speakers and she started nodding her head like this was her shit. When the song started, I wanted to turn that shit off because she was fucking up a classic cause she sounded horrible.

It could all be so simple, but you'd rather make it hard. Loving you is like a battle and we both end up with scars. Tell me, who I have to be, to get some reciprocity. No one loves you more than me, and no one ever will! Is this just a silly game, that forces you to ac...

I was saved by the damn bell when my phone started ringing. I went to reach for it but instead she grabbed it and answered.

"I know I dialed the wrong number." I shook my head when I heard my aggravating ass sister Shay.

"What you want Shailen?" I asked as Kewyn turned the phone to me.

"Oh shit! Corey, Corey! Get yo ass in here! Adonis has some woman answering his phone. And she pretty too! Nigga I don't know if she fine from her face and why the fuck yo ass care? Don't you have a woman?" Kewyn fell out laughing.

"His ass over there? What you and Corrupt doing together?" I asked.

"They came over to do his girl hair and she went run to the ATM." Shay replied.

"Please hang up on her ass." I damn near whispered.

"You better not tell her to hang up on me! What's your name?" Shay asked.

"Kewyn." She answered.

"You and my brother dating or just fucking?" Shay asked and Kewyn thought that shit was funny as fuck because she damn near fell out her seat laughing.

"Neither, I don't even like him." She said rolling her eyes once she got herself together.

"True. True, me either. Adonis what time will your plane land?" She called out to me and I stared at the road because I hadn't even told Kewyn her ass was leaving the state of Louisiana.

"What plane?" Kewyn asked.

"Get yo messy ass off the phone." I heard Corrupt call from the background.

"Oops, my bad. Brother, I love you and have a safe flight. Can't wait to meet you Kewyn!" Shay said hanging up the phone.

"Adonis, what plane?" Kewyn asked again.

"Mine." I answered.

"Yeah, but why are we going on a plane?" She didn't seem too upset about it.

"Shit, I ain't want to drive." I said shrugging my shoulders. "Let me ask you something, why are you okay with this whole situation?"

"I needed a breather." She said shrugging. "I figure that you may be just the breath of fresh air I needed so what was the point in complaining. I'll simply enjoy the couple of days in your presence until it was time to go home." I nodded my head at her answer. After that, we fell into a comfortable silence. I laughed to myself thinking of how pressed I was. Did I really just agree to front that lil nigga some work just to be in the presence of his sister? Hell yeah I did. I didn't have one regret about that shit either. Looking over, I noticed she started nodding off and the way her bottom lip dropped as if it was too heavy was sexy as fuck. "Stop watching me, creep." She said though her eyes were closed.

"Ain't nobody watching your ass." I replied, laughing because I was busted.

"Yes you were, I could feel your eyes on me. Just like I did in the restaurant. Leave me alone, I'm tired." She said before turning to face the door and shoving her legs underneath her body. I wanted to complain about her damn knees in my seat but the way her ass was peeking out from over her jeans made me give her a pass. Pulling into the airport, I parked as close to the strip as I could before climbing out the car and stretching my legs.

"How was the ride?" Jason, the guy who checked the plane asked.

"Too damn long." I replied laughing. The hour and a half wouldn't have been that bad if Kewyn's ass wasn't snoring loud as fuck. Her ass must have been tired because I drove over the shoulder a few times trying to *accidently* wake her ass up. "We ready to go?" I asked peering up at the plane. I couldn't wait until I was able to get my own instead of chartering this shit.

"Yep, waiting on you." He answered, I simply nodded my head.

"Cool, cool. My bags are in the trunk." I said handing him the key to the truck. Normally, I would have carried my own bag. I wasn't a nigga with a lil change who felt Hollywood or anything like that. Its just that today, I was carrying on something more valuable than that damn Louis Vuitton duffle bag. Walking over to the passenger side of the truck, I made sure she wasn't laying on the door before I opened it. Sliding my hands underneath her, I scooted her closer to me before lifting her up like she was a damn baby and carried her to the plane. As usual, the shit was spotless, and I was reminded why I never flew commercial if I could help it. I nodded at the pilot and some of his crew before taking a seat with Kewyn on my lap. After running through all of the preflight shit, we were on our way to Miami.

~

"THIS IS YOUR HOUSE?" Kewyn asked as we pulled up to my house.

"Yep. Come this way." I said walking up the stairs. Once we made it to the second floor, her mouth damn near hit the ground. The entire hallway was filled with windows that were wide open. The view over the beach was amazing and even I still stared in awe from time to time.

"This sunset. It's so beautiful." She spoke in a quiet voice. I left her standing there as I walked into my room and headed to the bathroom. Washing my hands, I went over how I was going to break the news to her that this wasn't what she thought it was. I wasn't sending her home after a day or two because how would that change anything. Her brother would have her safely, so he could simply run off with my product. Of course, I would find him and kill him, but I didn't want to give myself extra work. In order for me to trust him I needed to see how he moved this first batch and if the numbers added up. Until then, his sister could get real comfortable. Making my way out of the bathroom, I realized that would have to be a discussion for another time. Kewyn had climber her ass in my bed and was on her way back to sleep. That shit didn't sound too bad so I hopped in with her.

5

Shay

The hardest thing I have ever had to do in my life was watch the man I loved, loving on the next dusty ass bitch. From the age of 16, my heart was beating outside of my body. That nigga had my heart in his pocket and let him tell it, I had his. If that was the case, why the fuck was I sitting here in my salon waiting on his bitch to return from the bank? Corey and I went far back because he and my brother went far back, and I was always following them around when they weren't in the streets. Falling for him was easy, we vibed on a different level than I did from dudes my age. What was hard was knowing that he loved me but between his respect for my brother and jail time, because his ass was 19 going on 20, we had to sneak around and hide our shit. I guess after a couple of years the hiding got old because he was ready to tell my brother and I wasn't. I understood that I was finally legal, but I was still scared of what Adonis would say. Corey felt like us keeping it on the low made it seem like he was scared of my brother, but I still just wasn't ready. In return, he decided to test the fucking waters. I could have killed that nigga when he brought a random bitch to our house for dinner, but I couldn't. I had to play it cool because my brother was there. On some get back shit I started publicly dating this dude named Marcus. Yeah, we were both messing with people's hearts but that was a small price to pay if it got us back to each other, right? The shit didn't even work because not to long after I met Marcus, Corey went away to help Adonis handle some shit in another state. We didn't keep in touch but that did little to fade the feelings that I had for him. Fast forward a few years and here we were today.

"How you been Shy?" Corrupt asked, calling me by the name he gave me. I was so say sweeping hair from the floor but there was none. I just needed something to do with my hands.

"It's Shay and I'm good. I see you doing well." I said a little above a whisper, looking everywhere but at him. This was the reason only he could call me Shy. He was the only person that saw the side of me that wasn't all loud and in your face. How could I be as comfortable with a man as I was with him and yet I still was a ball of nerves when it was just he and I?

"You Shay to everyone else but look at you now. Look at me Shailen, I'm over here not on the fucking floor. Yo ass been sweeping the same area for ten damn minutes, ain't that much dirt in the world." He demanded. Looking up, I felt my face flush as I stared in his eyes. I wonder if he saw all the love I had for him through my eyes because I damn sure could see that shit in his. Before I could stop myself, I looked away again. "See what I'm talking about. This why your name going to forever be Shy to me. How yo bold ass in here with neon green hair but acting shy?" He laughed.

"Corey, we both know that I know the real you. Why you sent that girl to the bank when I can bet my last dollar that you have at least four stacks in cash, sitting in your pocket now." I said, saving the broom. When he started laughing, I shook my head because I knew he was on some bullshit.

"Shit, I wanted to run it with you, alone. See how you been and what's good with you and shit." He said walking, closer to me. I wanted him to stop where he was because I didn't have the strength to turn down any of his advances. I was strong as hell, probably one of the strongest women you've ever met. I've been through shit that would cause the strongest man to fold, without even breaking a sweat. With Corey, none of that mattered. I was so damn fragile when it came to him. I let my eyes roam over the face of the only man I would ever love. His beautiful brown eyes were set underneath a pair of bushy eyebrows. I remember hoping our future children got that from him. The way his mustache and bushy beard perfectly framed his beautiful, full lips reminded me of the many times they tickled my most intimate area when he ate it like he was starving. My eyes traced the tattoo that sat right at the lining of his wild and curly hair. If only they knew what the meaning behind that tattoo was.

"I'm good. I'm just out here doing what I have to do to make my brother proud." I said shrugging.

"Shit, you don't wanna make me proud too?" He asked, smirking.

"I did, at one point. Corey, leave me alone man. I ain't going down that road with you. Get gone before I have to beat Mika the fuck up." I said pointing in his face. He laughed and grabbed my hand that was in his face and pulled my body into his. When his arms wrapped around my body, I melted on the spot. Corey wasn't one of these small niggas, he was thick, and I loved that shit. I felt so protected in his arms.

"You know I still love the fuck out of your ass, right?" He whispered in my ear.

"Yeah, and I still love you too. I just know that its really time to let you go Corey. We not replaying that episode again." I spoke the words that broke my heart, as I pulled away from his embrace. Taking a few steps back, I knew we needed space in between us. I saw the affect that my words had on him, but I wouldn't take them back. I had been thinking it since I found out he was coming back here. He had Mika and I had a situation too. This was for the best.

"What you mean let it go?" He asked, frowning his bushy brows.

"On some Mariah Carey shit, when you left I dead ass lost a part of me. I physically cried until I was sick, often. I had to force myself to eat, I couldn't sleep, and I lost so much weight that I didn't recognize myself. My hair was falling out in patches, and you want to know what was the worst part about it all? The worst part was that, I had to silently drag myself back from the dead because no one knew what I was going through. I had to fake a smile any time I was in the presence of family and friends. Do you know how crazy you can drive yourself by smiling and laughing on the outside while you are physically falling to pieces underneath it all. Right before people's eyes I was losing my sanity, and no one cared because they didn't know. No one knew about us but you, and you left. You left out of my life like I meant nothing to you. Like it was easy to just say fuck Shay and the bond we created. I didn't want another nigga to touch me if it wasn't your touch. I didn't want another nigga to look my way, if it wasn't your beautiful brown eyes looking back. I didn't want a nigga to speak to me if it wasn't your voice that called out. You hurt me Corey. You hurt me so bad. You never reached out, you changed your number on me too." I said as a stray tear fell from my eye. I refused to let anymore fall though.

"Shy, I wasn't about to be someone's secret. I loved you then just like I love you now. You were too good to be a secret to any man, even me. When I started seeing other people, it was supposed to be a wake up call to you. I never wanted anyone but your stubborn ass. I still don't want anyone but your stubborn ass. Say the word and Mika is gone. That shit between us ain't hitting for nothing anyway. Let me do what I've always wanted. Let me put a ring on your finger and a thug ass nigga in your life." I listened as he poured out his heart and wanted to accept his offer so bad. Just as I took a step toward him the bell above the door rang, alerting us that someone was walking in.

"Shay, Baby?" I heard Mika call for both of us and I quickly wiped my face.

"You're too late." I whispered lifting my hand, so he could see the ring on my ring finger. He fucked up and another nigga lucked up.

"Girl you are bomb, I have gotten at least five compliments already. I was a little worried about this platinum blonde but you slayed me honey. Sorry I took so long, traffic." Mika explained handing me a roll of money. "What y'all doing?" She asked, looking at both of us.

"Umm. I was just showing Corey my ring. He was away when I got married and he didn't know." I replied, because Corey wasn't going to. His ass looked stuck as he stared at my hand with disgust.

"Ooooh congrats! It's a pretty ring! I hope I can get one like that soon." She hinted while smirking at Corey. "What's wrong with him?" She asked finally noticing his mug.

"Between him and Adonis, I don't know who thinks they run my life more. He isn't happy, I knew he wouldn't be. Anyway, I hope you get one soon too." I lied through my damn teeth.

"Let's go Mika. You ain't getting no damn ring like that. That shit would never touch the finger of a woman I planned on marrying. That lil ass ring proves that the marriage won't last." His ignorant ass said. I'm sure my facial expression matched Mika's and a fly could fly straight into my mouth because it had fallen open.

"That's the stupidest thing you've ever said and trust me you say a lot of stupid shit. Get your ass out of my shop so I can go home to my husband!" I said adding emphasis on the word husband. "Mika nice meeting you, call me when its time to touch your hair up and I got you. Don't leave Corey waiting too long, he's good at leaving people." I said, folding my arms. Mika looked confused and I felt bad for putting her in the middle of this bullshit. I heard the door to the shop close and quickly made sure everything was unplugged before turning off the lights. Walking out, I locked the doors and made my way to my 2017 matte black Benz GLS. I loved my truck and the fact that it still looked brand spanking new was the proof of that. Pulling off, I rode in silence as my mind drifted back to Corey. Lord knows I loved that man, I probably always would. But something was telling me that it was time to close that chapter. Hell, my ring was telling me it was time to close the entire damn book and put it on the shelf. What we shared was special to me, but I had to leave it in the past. Something told me that Corey wasn't going to leave well enough alone though. Pulling up home, I grabbed the mail then made my way inside.

"You're late and there's no dinner." Malcolm said as a greeting as soon as I walked through the door. Instead of answering his ass, I flipped through the mail and threw the new take out menus on the table in front of him.

"Don't hurt yourself with all the options pimp." I said popping the p as I made my way to our bedroom. I looked at the picture that hung above the head board and rolled my eyes. I was in a beautiful Vera Wang wedding gown and Malcolm looked handsome in an all black tuxedo on our wedding day. Back then, I wasn't even sure if I was in love with Malcolm. Now, I was sure that I wasn't. Marrying him was a way for me to cope with the void that I felt, and I was on some get back from my brother.

"If you want longevity in our marriage, this isn't the way you go about proving that to me, Shailen." I rolled my eyes as he said my name. I swear on a stack of bibles the way he said it all hard and shit made me sick. "You can start by making it home in a decent amount of time so that your household duties aren't forgotten." He added, walking further into the room.

"Malcolm, my daddy is dead! I don't need another one. Watch how you talk to me, bruh. I was working at the shop and I came as soon as I was done. You've been home for what, at least two hours, right? Seems like that was enough fucking time for you to cook two meals if you wanted to." I snapped.

"I don't even know why your brother got you that shop. You haven't even graduated your lil hair school yet so that idea wasn't the smartest. Besides, as the woman its your job to cook an

9d clean. That's how my parents run their household and that's how I'll rune mine also." I turned in his direction so quick, I felt my neck crack.

"Boy, fuck your mama and daddy, the fuck! Look, it seems like we can never be on the same page so maybe we should discuss different options. If you aren't happy with me as a woman and I'm not happy with you as a man, maybe we would be happier apart. Oh, and he got me the shop because he knows the potential I have. Don't make me call my brother and let him know you said he was stupid." I know I was petty for saying that, but he knew better than to speak on Adonis.

Adonis didn't fuck with his ass at all and he knew that shit! I didn't wait for his reply because my body was crying to be submerged in the powerful stream of the jets in the bathtub. I walked into the bathroom and ran my water while dumping some bath salts and bubble bath in it. Not even waiting for the tub to fill up, I stripped and slid in the water. The little disagreement Malcom and I had was no longer on my mind. Its not that the argument was forgotten or anything, it was just that my mind was too clouded with thoughts of Corey to think of anything else.

6

Kewyn
Stretching my arms above my head, I was greeted with an amazing scent. Call me fat all you want, but I was sure I smelled eggs, bacon and blueberry pancakes. No, no that was waffles. The sound of my stomach growling reminded me that I hadn't ate anything the previous night. At least, I thought it was another day. The curtains in the room canceled out any light from outside, if there was even any. I looked around for my phone and found it on the nightstand still powered off. Holding down the button to power it on, I knew I was about to get a shitload of texts and voice-mails from Ty and Dez wondering what was going on with me. After waiting a few moments, the joke was on me. I had two funky ass text messages, one from each of them. I clicked on Dez's text first and rolled my damn eyes at her weak ass apology and explanation.

Dez: I'm sorry about how things went down bae. You will understand that this was all done for us. At the end of the day, I want you happy. I love you so much that the shit is scary.

Me: You sure have a funny way of showing that. There is a lot we need to talk about when I come back later on today.

I saw she read it and within seconds, the bubbles appeared letting me know that she was responding.

Dez: Like I said, you will understand when this is all said and done. Once you talk to Don today, please don't hate me. Remember, this was all done for the both of us. I know you'll need your time to cope, but I'll be here when you are finally ready to talk.

When she said that, I was immediately confused. Talk to Don about what? What did I need time to cope with?

Me: ????? What are you talking about (Thinking Emoji)

I noticed she read it before the bubbles appeared again. They blinked for a few moments before disappearing. I watched them return and disappear again and after looking at the screen for five minutes, I realized she either couldn't or just wasn't going to respond. Exiting her text thread, I clicked on the one for Ty and found myself getting pissed off.

Ty: You thought that shit was real cute huh, bitch? Let's see if you feel that way after your lil time away from home.

Bitch? Ty had never spoken to me like that ever. What the fuck type of shit was he on? I clicked on his contact but before I could press the call button near his name, there was a soft knock on the door. I stared in the direction of the door but didn't say anything. I mean, why would I? It's his damn house and his room so I'm sure he didn't need permission to enter. Instead of the door opening, there was another knock.

"Umm, come in." I skeptically called out. Seconds later the door swung open and in walked his sister, Shay. I recognized her from the facetime call in the car. There was no way I would be forgetting the beautiful dark chocolate woman with the lime green extensions. I was shocked that I actually loved the look. On her, anyway. There was no way I would be able to pull off something like that.

"Hey girl, Kewyn, right?" She asked walking in the room with shopping bags.

"Yeah, you can call me Key. That hair is even louder in person." I said laughing. I knew she wasn't offended because she spun around as if she was modeling.

"Ain't it though? I needed a color and style that said, I'm here bitches and I ain't to be fucked with." She said laughing and placing the bags on the bed. "These are for you. You have underclothes, accessories, a couple dresses, some jeans, couple blouses, t shirts, thot wear, lingerie if you feeling freaky, personal hygiene shit, oh I didn't know if you were the conservative type or if you were bout that life so I grabbed a bunch of heels, tennis shoes, makeup and some bundles cause I'm getting all up in that head on today, lounge wear and a lil bit of makeup. I guessed your foundation and concealer color cause I'm really good at that, but my brother gave me your clothing sizes." She said using her fingers to count off the shit she said. Now, I liked to shop like the next person, so I jumped to see if her style was up to par. Looking through the bags, I fell in love with e-v-e-r-y-t-h-i-n-g! From the shoes, to the expensive jewelry on down to the clothes. I wanted to wear all this shit today. NOW! When I looked up at Shay she was smiling and nodding her head. "Uh huh, give a bitch her props. I got skills huh?" She gloated.

"Yeah, you good at what you do! But why? Why did you get all of this?" I asked confused.

"Oh baby, Shay likes her money too much to spend on anyone but Shay. Adonis definitely took care of all of this." She replied whipping out a black card. I had never seen one of those bitches and I'm sure I drooled just looking at this one.

"But why did he get me all of this? I should be leaving today or tomorrow, right?" I turned my statement into a question because of the look that graced her face.

"I didn't get that impression. In fact, this was just to hold you off until you went into the stores for yourself. Look, I didn't ask many questions because as soon as he handed me the card, I was thinking about the shit I would cop myself. Wait until you see these bad ass Yves Saint Laurent heels I have, hell I copped you the same pair in red." She rambled but my mind was wondering.

"Wait, rewind for a second or two. Exactly how long did he say that he thought, I was staying here?" I asked adding emphasis on thought. They obviously had me fucked up.

"He didn't. He just didn't sound like you were leaving anytime soon. Look, I don't know what's going on but you can ask him. He's in the gym working out." She said digging in one of the bags and grabbing a shitload of weave.

"Wait, I'm not wearing all of that." I said, momentarily distracted.

"I know you ain't, some of this is mine. Baby, you can't handle thirty inches of this luxurious shit yet. I got you 22 inches. Oh, but stick around and I'll have your ass on this Nicki Minaj and Cardi B shit too!" She laughed.

"I doubt that!" I responded. "Where is the gym?" I asked finally climbing out of the massive bed.

"Down the stairs, take the first right, keep straight down that long hallway and it'll be to your left. Just a warning, he is usually in a zone and hates when he gets interrupted." I could care less about what his ass hated. I needed answers and I wanted them now. I looked down at my yesterday clothing and almost wanted to postpone this. Almost.

"I'll be right back." I said walking out of the room and following her directions. Although the house was big, I found the gym with no problems thanks to the loud ass trap music that was playing. It wasn't what I expected to see though. In my mind, I would see some machines and a basketball court. Instead, there was a huge boxing ring with machines positioned around it. Adonis and some big bright guy were both in the boxing ring punching a couple of punching bags. He was cute, but my eyes were on Adonis. This man was rightfully named. His body was nothing short of amazing and I couldn't seem to look away from it. He was shirtless, but he was rocking a pair of basketball shorts with some compression tights underneath them. I could even see the muscles in his damn legs.

"Aye bruh, we got company." The bright guy screamed over the music, getting Adonis' attention. I could tell he was mixed with something, I just didn't know what. I could also tell his ass was nothing to be played with.

"You finally up?" Adonis asked climbing out of the ring. He grabbed a towel and wiped his face then his chest and bitch, I never wanted to be a towel so bad in my whole damn life.

"Yeah, I didn't realize just how tired I was." I said, nervously giggling.

"You ate?" He asked, peering into my eyes.

"Not yet, I was talking to Shay." I explained.

"Shay here?" The bright dude asked getting out the ring also. I noticed Adonis stare at him for a second.

"Why you want to know?" He asked.

"Her ass said she was going braid my hair, I need to see when." He responded, and Adonis stared at him for a few more seconds. I could tell he was lying but obviously Adonis didn't.

"Corrupt, this is Kewyn. Kewyn This my right hand Corrupt." He introduces us as his eyes found mine again.

"Nice to meet you." I responded but my eyes never left Corrupts face. The way he stared back into my eyes made it hard for me to look away. I heard Corrupt chuckle.

"Nice to meet yo ass too but you ain't worried about me. You all in Don fucking face." Corrupt laughed and I felt myself blush. For a fraction of a second, I saw a smirk on Adonis' face.

"Umm, can I talk to him for a second?" I nervously asked.

"Yeah, let me holla at sis." He said, looking at Adonis as he said the word sis. I waited for him to walk out before I stated the reason I came down here.

"First of all, thank you for the clothing and all the rest of the things. You didn't have to do that, so I appreciate it." I started.

"I know I didn't have to do anything. You are welcome." He replied.

"Umm, I'm appreciative but don't you think you did too much? Like, I'm only here for maybe today and tomorrow." I said. I didn't want to come right out and ask him how long I was here for because I was sure I would be going home soon. He didn't immediately answer and that bothered me. Instead, he leaned back on a piece of machinery and strokes his beard. The whole time, his eyes studied mine.

"Did you speak with your brother and his girl?" He asked.

"Who?" I replied then it hit me. "Oh Ty and Dez? Not yet. What's going on? You look like you holding something back." I said a lil louder than I realized. Pushing himself up from the machine, he stepped closer to me.

"Alright ma, I'm just goin say it because no matter how I try to clean it up the shit goin sound all wrong. Your brother and his girl needed me to front them some work, kind of like a test trial. In order to do some shit like that, I have to trust you. I trust two people in my life, and they upstairs. They decided to send you here until they moved the supply I gave them. After that, they'll have their re-up money and they won't need to use you as a bargaining tool. So, to answer your unasked question, you can go home when I get paid in full." He finished like it was nothing.

"No. Dez said a fucking date! One fucking date! That was all I agreed to. If you need someone to stay until they move all that shit, go get Dez. I will keep my word, so like I said its one date and I'm gone. Whether you bring me back or I leave on my own, I'm going back home!" I stated before turning and storming out. If someone saw me they would think I was going crazy as I talked aloud to myself on my way back to the room. "A fucking bargaining tool! I'm nobody's fucking bargaining tool! They got me fucked all the way up. Watch me nut the fuck up in this bitch. Show they asses that they not about to play with me!" Busting back through the bedroom door, I noticed that Corrupt and Shay seemed to be in the middle of an argument, but I paid them no mind. Grabbing my cell phone, I stomped to the bathroom and slammed the door behind me. I hit the call button next to Dez's name so fucking hard that I broke a nail against the screen.

"I'm so sorry!" She answered the phone attempting to explain.

"Nah bitch! You ain't sorry yet! Pack your fucking bags because when I come home tomorrow, tag your it! You need to come stay with Adonis over here til Ty bitch ass moves that shit! And then after that, make sure this nigga gives you some bread so you can get a spot with Ty cause I ain't fucking with either of y'all after this lame shit. How the fuck you a female fuck boy?" I spazzed before hanging up in her face. Bruh I wish we still used them damn phones that was hooked to the wall. Slamming that bitch down in some hoe's face was more effective than a simple call ended. I sat down on the toilet for at least ten minutes trying to calm the fuck down. No matter how much you love someone or they love you, people always seem to disappoint a motherfucker. Ty and Dez knew all I had in this world were them. I didn't fuck with my family, long story but I didn't. I loved Dez but I knew ending things with her was the easier task. Ty and I, we had history. We had each other back when all we had were each other. No matter how much I knew I had outgrown what we had, loyalty told me not to go despite my heart saying run. Picking up my phone again, I finally called him.

"Yo!" He answered sounding weird.

"Yo? That's all you have to say to me? You didn't even call to make sure nothing happened to me Tyreek! You and Dez offered me up to a complete fucking stranger like I ain't mean shit to y'all bruh!" I was talking in a harsh whisper. Because I didn't know who was on the other side of the door.

"Maaaaan look, a nigga don't wanna hear all that Key. That's why shit wasn't working between us, all the fuck you do is nag." He paused and I heard him talk as if the phone was no longer to his ear. His voice sounded a lil more distant. "Aye, hop on and remind me why I fuck with you the way I do." He said before coming back. "What was I saying? Oh yeah, you would make a nigga happy if you just learn how to relax shawty. Calm the fuck... Shiiiiittttt, just like that ma!" He moaned into the phone.

"Nigga, nigga are you fucking while we talking?" I asked not believing this shit. He didn't say anything, but I definitely heard a bitch moaning loud and clear.

"Hang up and focus on this pussy." She damn near whispered.

"Aye, you heard what she said. I gotta go!" He spoke into the phone and then the nigga really hung up on me. Her voice sounded off but I'm positive that nigga was fucking Dez and they both just played me! I sat there so mad that tears rolled down my face. I literally had to hug myself so that I wouldn't punch holes in Adonis' wall. I had been more than the perfect woman to both of them and this was how they repaid me. Yeah, just wait until tomorrow. I was flying straight into Lafayette, fuck renting a car in New Orleans. When I touched down, it was to cause nothing but hell. Instead of walking out of the rest room, I stripped and got into the state of the art shower. The bath and body works that Shay had grabbed for me was already in the shower so I assume she saved all of the items. I grabbed three wash cloths from the closet on side of the shower and let the water cascade down my body. I needed to wash my hair since Shay wanted to do it and I was glad she had brought shampoo and conditioner that I liked. After washing my face with one towel, I used a second on my body with the Bath and Body Works and the third I used between my legs with some of the dial body wash that was in the shower. I didn't want to use his items, but I was not catching a damn yeast infection from passing all that fragrance filled shit between my legs. After I finished washing off, I wrapped a body towel around my body and another around my hair while I brushed my teeth. I could tell his ass damn sure didn't buy towels from Walmart, these were so plush that I wanted to take some home with me.

"I thought you would never come out." Shay said plugging blow dryers and flat irons up. She had converted the area that was used for sitting into a damn mini salon. "You ok?" She asked, looking genuinely concerned.

"I will be as soon as I get home tomorrow." I replied. I noticed she looked at me like I was crazy.

"Umm Kee Kee, that's what I'm going to call you. Anyway, my brother may seem all cool calm and collected but that shit came from a lot of years of counseling and meds. That nigga crazy baby. You not leaving unless he says that you're leaving." She said laughing. "I love him, but he is a bit of a control freak. Trust me, I know. His ways is the reason I'm unhappily married." She said and made a face like the last part slipped out.

"Is that also the reason you and Corrupt hide the fact that y'all fucking?" I asked folding my arms and looking her in the eyes. Her ass dropped the curling wand she was holding and ran to the door, swung it open and looked both ways into the hallway.

"Bitch, are you crazy. Don't say no shit like that! Corrupt is like a brother to me." She lied.

"Then that's like incest. How long y'all been fucking?" I asked.

"Look, I'll treat you to lunch and fill you in. What we ain't going do is talk about that where my brother can hear that shit though. What Corrupt and I had, is over. I'm married." She said flashing her ring. The shit was actually too small for a person with her personality but whatever.

"You keep saying that until you believe it, ok? The way Corrupt eyes lit up when he realized you were here, the way you too were staring at each other when I burst in and the way you didn't make eye contact when you said that last lil spill, lets me know you have some shit on your hands. He doesn't seem to agree with that lie you said, and you don't either." I said removing the towel from my head.

"Come sit down so I can get you ready for tonight. I have to get myself ready too. We are all going to the club after y'all get back from dinner." I didn't say anything as I did as she instructed. I would enjoy their world tonight because tomorrow I was heading back to my own.

7

A donis

"I shouldn't have brought her ass in the bitch. Watch she be the cause of some old ass hoe crying over a coffin next weekend." I said aloud, throwing back a shot of D'usse.

"Nigga, I see the fire dancing in your eyes." Corrupt said laughing. We were leaning over the bar of the vip area while watching the girls dance on the dance floor below us. When we went to dinner, Kewyn was dressed in a red fitted gown that fell to her knees. Though her ass was on Texas in it, she couldn´t help that she was blessed. Plus, I wasn't tripping too much because it was a private dinner with just us two. I fucked up when she requested that I swung home to let her change into something more club appropriate. Instead of getting down, I sat in the car and handled business. Her clothes had to have been picked out before we left because she was in and out. I was too into my phone to check her out and the car was dark anyway. By time I realized that her ass was halfway naked, we were already here. A nigga wanted to push her back in the car and pull off, but I didn't want to scare her lil ass. She probably already thought I was a fucking kidnapper.

"I'm going fuck Shay up." I said aloud while shaking my head.

"What Shy do?" Corrupt asked.

"She brought that damn outfit. Kewyn too damn fine for that." I answered with my eyes trained on her. Shay, Mika and Kewyn were on the dance floor twerking to some Migos song and Shay ratchet ass had Kewyn drinking from the bottle. She went from rocking from side to side when we first got here to scrapping the damn ground with her ass. She must have felt my eyes burning a hole through her body because as soon as she stopped drinking from the bottle, her eyes were on me. She stared me down for a few moments until a sexy smirk covered her face. She tapped Shay and Mika then whispered in their ear as she handed her the bottle. Shay laughed obnoxiously before looking up at me and shaking her head with a huge smile. I didn't have to wonder what was going on for long because Mika went into her purse and pulled out a stack of money as Kewyn turned her back and put on a show that I knew was for my pleasure. The music was now on Waka Flaka old joint, Round of Applause. Kewyn's ass was down there putting on a show as Mika made it rain on her and Shay slapped her ass. I swear on my mama, that ass had a mind of its own. There were plenty of women on the dance floor but Shay had all eyes on here. After a while, Mika started dancing too. Now Kewyn had a fat ass but Mika had a different kind of fat ass. You could tell that shit was fake but hey, she wasn't my concern. I was just a lil bit stuck on why that shit wasn't moving right.

"Nah, I'm going down there." Corrupt said walking toward the stairs. I followed his lead and made my way to the women too. Once we got downstairs I didn't see them.

"Where they at?" I asked one of my lil niggas I had watching them.

"At the bar. Ms. New Booty drunk as shit too." He said laughing.

"Nigga, was you looking at her ass?" I asked massaging my temples.

"I mean boss man, everyone was looking at her ass." He said with a shrug. I walked closer to him to ensure he heard me.

"When you see that ass, play Stevie Wonder to that shit before I make you Stevie Wonder like. Cool?" I asked.

"Big bet! I didn't know that was you man. My bad, you know I would never violate." He apologized. I didn't offer him another word because I looked over and saw some niggas in the girl's faces. Corrupt saw the look on my face before we turned and headed in their direction.

"I'm saying ma, what a nigga gotta do to be with you tonight?" I heard one of them spitting game to Kewyn. I set back a lil bit because I wanted to see how she would handle herself. When she wrapped her arm around his neck I found myself getting disappointed. After the way we vibed at dinner, I didn't take her for some cheap thrill. She carried herself better than that.

"You wanna be with me tonight, boo?" She asked. That nigga almost broke his neck nodding.

"You wanna fuck tonight?" She asked pissing me off.

"Hell yeah!" That nigga replied nodding even harder. His home-boys clapped hands with him. I noticed one of them had their arms wrapped around Shay's waist.

"I can make that happen." Kewyn replied before her eyes met mine then she turned back to him. "All you gotta do is grow a lil bit, you like 6'1 and the nigga I want to fuck is likeeeee." She paused before turning to look at me again. "6'4 give or take an inch." She replied looking back at him. "You a lil too bright too. This nigga skin so dark I think he's the new king of Wakanda. Matter of fact, when he fucks me tonight, I'm calling that nigga T'challa!" I couldn't help but to fall out laughing and I noticed I wasn't alone. Corrupt was dying laughing and Shay and Mika had all fallen over the bar laughing at Kewyn. What was even more funnier was that her face was dead ass serious. She looked around like she didn't know what was funny. When I walked over to her laughing she looked confused. "What Adonis? What's funny? I am going call you that tonight and you going call me Nakia, huh?" She asked and I swear we lost our shit again because her ass was really waiting on an answer. The liquor had lil mama gone.

"Whatever you want ma." I replied still laughing.

"Can we leave now? I got some things I want to do to you." She said. I think she thought it came off as a whisper but we all heard her.

"Bitch, how you went from saying you didn't want to be here to saying you want to do some things to my brother? He a virgin hoe, you ain't going take advantage of my baby!" Shay said laughing her ass off.

"Then I'm going pop his cherry. T'challa going be hooked on phonics when I'm done with him. You know they say you never get over your first." Kewyn said with her lips poked out. Before I could answer, Corrupt spazzed.

"Aye, why the fuck you niggas still standing right there laughing like this shit is Def Comedy Jam? Move the fuck around." He roared.

"No disrespect, I didn't know they were with anyone." The one that was trying to talk to Kewyn said.

"Oh, I'm not with any of them. That's my brother and that angry one is his lil friend." Shay said. Corrupt head snapped in her direction quick as shit. I'm sure he felt played behind that lil friend comment.

"So, can I have your number?" The nigga asked her.

"No the fuck you can't!" Corrupt said before I could say anything. Shit I wasn't really focused on them no way because Kewyn had grabbed one of those liquor infused lollipops from the bartender and was going to work on that shit.

"Why he can't Corrupt? Huh? Last time I checked, Mika was your woman. Go boss her the fuck around." Shay snapped. I don't even know why the fuck she played with Corrupt, he really felt like she was his sister. For as long as I could remember that nigga been running niggas away from her. He felt like no nigga was good enough for her. I remember one time, one of our homeboys made the mistake of stepping to me and asked to take her out on a date. Corrupt shut that nigga down and he was pissed because of that. Nigga told Corrupt mind his business because he saw the way he looked at Shay and he knew he wanted her. Corrupt flashed out and beat the fuck out of Gil. That nigga was in a fucking coma for a few weeks before they pulled the plug on his ass. Wasn't no coming back from what Corrupt did to him. When I asked him why the fuck he was so mad, he let me know that he loved Shay just as much as I did. Nigga actually said more than I did but we both knew he was tripping. I knew that it was because she was as close to him as she was to me.

"Man, go head on Shy. Your ass married! Ain't that's what you said earlier?" He asked.

"Shit, what that nigga don't know won't hurt him. Any way baby, let me see your phone." She said stretching out her hand. The nigga passed her the phone, obviously not giving a fuck that she was married. After a few seconds she passed it back. Dude couldn't even pocket his shit before Corrupt had his glock pulled out.

"If you want to walk out that door alive, run me that phone." Corrupt calmly said. I knew when that nigga was calm that, that was grounds to worry.

"Baby, you are doing too much! Shay is a grown woman, she can do what she wants." Mika said.

"Shut the fuck up Mika. Shy ain't fucking with none of these busta ass niggas. When she choses to fuck with a real nigga, then I'll calm down." He said. "RUN ME THAT FUCKING PHONE!" He roared. A few people around us moved around but I just shook my head. I never had to defend Shay cause this nigga always went above and beyond to handle shit. The nigga handed Corrupt his phone and I watched his big ass break this nigga iPhone with his bare hands before throwing it in a glass of liquor. "Beat your fucking feet." He told dude. Nigga listened too.

"Ohhhhh, I told your ass! I told your ass!" Kewyn said still thinking she was whispering. "T'challa, I'm faded and feeling X rated. It's Mr nasty time!" She said even making Corrupt ass laugh a lil bit.

"That shit was wack Corey!" Shay spat.

"Nah, that nigga was wack. He wasn't the one for you. I told you the type of nigga you need, sis." He said laughing. "Let's go Mika!" He said before walking away without saying bye to anyone else. I knew his ass was mad, but the shit was pointless. Shay always got to him and he just wouldn't understand that she was grown. As long as no one cause her harm, she was free to do her. After making sure Shay got in her car safely, I led the way to mine. Kewyn's ass was on ten as she rubbed on my dick and singing what sounded like Lion King songs.

"Man, what the fuck are you singing Kewyn?" I asked laughing.

"This that shit that was on The Black Panther. I'm setting the mood for us to role play." She said making me fall out laughing. I swear a nigga hasn't laughed like this, ever. All throughout dinner, the conversation just flowed. Nothing was forced and I'm sure I hurt myself laughing at her silly ass. I could tell that she wasn't hyped off of how fancy the restaurant was, or that I bought it out. She was more impressed with things like me pulling out her chair, helping her out of the car and opening doors. She was born and raised as far south as she could be but was still missing out on that southern charm. We spoke a lil about her past and mine, but I could tell from the way she paused ever so often that she was holding some shit back. I was very observant, so I noticed that she was hurt bad and that it was fresh and had cut her deep. I wanted more than anything to be there for her and to protect her but first she had to fully open up to me. Although she kept spitting that shit about going home, tonight her ass sat at that dinner table talking about all the shit she wanted to do in the city this weekend. Looking over, I noticed her drunk ass was talking cash money shit but now she was over there, sleep. Yep, with that loud ass snoring. I made it home in no time and after undressing myself and her, I hopped in the bed and pulled her close. Within seconds, I was out.

I FELT Kewyn sneaking out of the bed and sneak her ass around the room. Opening one eye, I watched her walk into the bathroom and as soon as she closed the door, I grabbed my cell phone and sent a message to a couple of my people. I heard the shower and couldn't help but to laugh, her ass thought she was leaving but I couldn't let that happen. I told her what it was and there wasn't anything that would change that. While the shower ran, I went to the safe that I had hidden in the room. It wasn't the main one in the house and I didn't keep much in it, but it would work for this. I knew that her ass didn't have money because I took her debit card and she complained about losing it yesterday. She was really trying to pay for her own dinner last night. I opened the safe a bit and left it exposed before getting back in bed just as the shower turned off. After a few minutes, she came out in a pair of black jeans, a fitted white tee and a pair of air max. She stared at me for a few seconds as if she was contemplating something before she turned away and grabbed her book sack purse. She looked towards the safe and back at me before fully opening it up. There was stacks of money in there, but I watched her pull out one stack and count a few bills out before placing the rest back. Then she went to the dresser, grabbed a pen and paper and scribbled a note. I watched as she placed it down and looked back towards me before finally leaving. For a few moments I lay there just in case she returned, but she didn't. I quickly got up and read the note.

Adonis,

In a perfect world, things wouldn't be so complicated between us. There are some things about me that you don't know, and I don't care to share. I just know that in the short amount of time that we spent talking over dinner, I knew you were special and deserved more than I could offer you right now or maybe not ever. I appreciate what you did for me but seeing that I'm not entertaining this whole use me as a bargaining tool bullshit, I felt it was more honest for me to leave behind the things you got me. Once I make it back home, I'll send you the money for the outfit I took with me as well as the hair. Also, I took $284 from your safe, it was the exact amount of my flight home. I'll pay that back too. Take care of yourself and let Shay know that I enjoyed her presence.

Kewyn

I sat there stunned for a second. It wasn't often that you ran into a woman that was made like Kewyn. This was some once in a lifetime shit. Yeah, I wasn't ready for shorty to leave and honestly, I wasn't sure I would ever be ready.

8

Shay

"Where are you going Shailen?" Malcolm asked, making me roll my eyes.

"To my brother's house. Why, are you coming?" I asked knowing he didn't go anywhere near Adonis.

"No, I was wondering if we could spend the day together and maybe grab some lunch. Then start on that family we talked about." He lost me as soon as he said family.

"I told you I wanted to have my career up and running before we decided on a family, Malcom." I said. I watched his face frown up and waited for him to explode.

"Fine, don't wait up for me tonight." He said as if I ever waited up for him. I didn't even respond. I finished getting ready and walked out of the house. Malcolm always said that shit hoping I would change my mind about whatever the hell I had just said. Wrong! I turned the volume up on the ready and blasted Yo Gotti, all the way to my brother's house. I didn't tell him I was coming because I wasn't coming for his ass. I was going to bring Kewyn with me to lunch. I was meeting my home girl Natasha and spill tea on Corrupt's ass, so I may as well tell Kewyn at the same time. Parking in front, I used my key to let myself in.

"Adonis! Kewyn!" I called out. I didn't know if I was interrupting things, so I was giving them a lil warning. I smelled food in the kitchen and I knew the chef always prepared some bomb meals. My stomach growled and even though we were going to lunch, I could nibble on something while I waited for them to come down. I made my way to the kitchen but stopped dead in my tracks in the dining room.

"Hey sis, I didn't know you were here." Adonis said with a smile as he shoved a piece of chicken in his mouth.

"I'm calling mama, like you dead ass tripping and I'm telling!" I spat pulling out my phone. His ass just shrugged me off, but he would be singing a different tune in a minute.

"Hey baby." My mama answered.

"Ma! Something is really wrong with your son." I said skipping over the pleasantries.

"What the hell did Adonis do now?" She asked giggling.

"Nothing funny, he got this girl taped to the freaking chair mama. Like she is legit duck taped to the dining room table." I said shaking my head. Looking at Kewyn, I could see that she was pissed off, but he truly looked unbothered.

"Put me on speaker phone!" She demanded. I did exactly what she asked me to. ADONIS JAILEN PARKS!" She roared.

"Ma, how are you beautiful? How is Cabo?" He asked like the shit he was doing was normal.

"Fuck Cabo, do you know that kidnapping is a crime nigga! Why do you have that poor girl taped to a damn chair? When Shay told me about this shit I wanted to give you the benefit of the doubt but nooooo, you gotta milk shit. Let her go!" she spat.

"I can't ma. She trying to leave and I ain't ready to let her go. Plus, I didn't even kidnap her ass. Some niggas did, and I saved her. She should be thanking me." He said walking over to Kewyn. He softly removed the tape from her mouth. "You want to thank me or no?"

"Fuck you Adonis! I wish the fuck I would say thank you. You made them niggas snatch me up and throw me in the fucking trunk. Nigga, I almost died! Untape me from this chair and watch what I do. What? You thought I was scared of yo ass? Untape me and see!" Kewyn spat. I could tell she was a lil feisty and I liked her for my brother.

"Oh damn. She told yo ass!" My mama said laughing. "Adonis, quit that crazy shit man, y'all cutting into my spa day. Let that girl go and once I get back next week, we will talk about this shit." She said hanging up the phone. As old as either of us were, ma dukes got that act right out of us.

"Since you want to snitch run me my damn card." Adonis said iffing at me.

"You can have your funky lil card, after me and Kewyn come back from lunch." I said.

"Kewyn ain't going nowhere bruh." He said, waving me off.

"Adonis, you can't just keep her taped to a chair. Let me take her to lunch and talk to her. I'm already knowing you going send some of your people to watch over us so she ain't gone leave bruh." I said rolling my eyes. Hell, to be honest, I didn't know if she would run again but I didn't care either. Adonis was tripping.

"We don't have to talk about anything, I'm going the fuck home." Kewyn spat.

"See, that's why her ass staying with me." He said with a shrug.

"And then what? What you going to do when you have to handle business?" I pulled him to the side away from Kewyn. "Let me talk to her, I'll convince her to stay man. You know I can!" I said.

"Mannnn. Don't play with me Shay! Her ass the only thing that's guaranteeing I get paid without catching a fucking body." He warned.

"Adonis, quit lying. You don't give a fuck about killing someone or that money. You just want her here with you, period. I get it but this ain't the way. Let her want to be here. She not going want to stay if she locked in the fucking house. Let her enjoy the city, I'm bringing her to meet Natasha so meeting new people will be good for her." I explained.

"Nah, Natasha ass don't sit right with me. I don't even want your ass with her." He said, and I rolled my eyes.

"Man, Natasha cool people. You just don't like her because you hit it and quit it and she was a lil bit of a stalker. She got over you and has a new boo so chill." I said walking away. I told Adonis to leave my friends alone, but he just had to fuck Natasha. I knew he didn't want anything serious and he told her so too. The thing is, Natasha the type of broad that thinks her pussy is as magical as a unicorn. She felt like she could change a grown ass man and failed. Adonis will walk past my friend like he never met her and that hurts her to her foundation. Long story short, she started popping up on his ass everywhere he went. When I say everywhere, I mean everywhere. Clubs, his house, my house, traps, church, yep church and even to the hospital when he was checking on one of his workers that had been shot. I had to put a stop to that shit and soon after she got involved with some man. I never met him because she didn't want to jinx it, but I was happy that he kept her happy and away from my brother.

"Kewyn when I let yo ass loose, you better keep your hands to yourself. I don't hit women but mama ain't said shit about pistol whipping you." He warned but I knew he wouldn't touch her. That nigga was hooked on Kewyn. I watched as he went in her purse, opened her wallet and snatched her cash and driver's license out. "Can't go nowhere without this." He replied before pocketing her shit. As soon as he removed the tape from her, she stood up and stretched. I knew her ass was too quiet, and I sat there waiting for her to make her move. After an exaggerated slap, she cocked back and punched the fuck out of Adonis. I figured she would slap him or something like that, but this bitch was nuts. I didn't even have the balls to do that shit. I quickly stood up to stop his ass before his anger got the best of him, but I was too late.

"Adonis, don't hit her!" I screamed as he charged at her. She wasn't that hard because she hauled ass and he was right behind her. When she turned to see where he was her dumb ass fell like the white girls in the movies and he snatched her ass up. I cringed when he lifter her off her feet by holding on to her arms and slammed her into the wall behind her. "Adonis, let her go!" I demanded.

"Shay, get the fuck out!" He roared. He ain't have to tell me twice. I said a prayer for my girl then hauled ass. I noticed that I had a text from Natasha and I clicked to open it.

Natasha: Can't stay late, I have a date with bae.

Me: I ain't mad at ya boo! Do you boo boo, do you! Kmsl

After responding, I went to check on Kewyn and my damn mouth fell open. This bitch had her legs wrapped around his waist and they were damn near eating each other's face. My brother was grinding in between her legs and I heard her moaning in his mouth. How the fuck did they go from wanting to kill each other to damn near making me an auntie.

"Y'all do that shit on y'all own time. Let's go Key Key!" I said, interrupting them. Her ass jumped down so quick I thought she was going to fall. I laughed because her face was red as fuck. Adonis ass didn't turn from the wall and I knew it was because he was trying to handle the hard on she left him with. That nigga was going to need a cold shower.

"Ummm, we will talk when I get back." She said smoothing her hair. Without another word, she grabbed her purse and walked out the house.

"See, she plans on coming back anyway." I said and followed her out. Her ass was silent the entire ride to the restaurant and I didn't bother her. Handing my keys to the valet, we made our way inside where I immediately saw Natasha. She was glowing, and I was happy for my friend. "Hey beautiful." I said walking over and kissing her cheek.

"Hey boo, who is your friend?" She asked looking at Kewyn.

"Oh, this is Kee Kee, and Kee this is Natasha." I made quick introductions between the two.

"Hey, I love that dress." Kewyn said complimenting the bright yellow maxi dress that Natasha was wearing.

"Thanks boo, I wish I would have come as comfortable as you are. I wouldn't have to wear heels." Natasha replied.

"Girl, you look great. If Adonis' ass would have left me alone, maybe I would have changed." Kewyn replied. I noticed Natasha shot a look her way and knew that this wouldn't go well.

"Oh, you're Adonis' new toy huh?" Natasha asked, throwing more shade than the clouds ever could. Kewyn surprised me when she laughed.

"Strike one." She said more so to herself.

"Anyway, I brought y'all here to talk about my issue." I said interrupting them.

"With Malcolm?" Natasha asked. Before I could answer, we paused to place our order.

"Girl, fuck Malcolm. My problem is with Corey." I said, and her mouth fell open.

"Wait, he's back?" She asked. I watched her toy with her phone for a second as I thought on how to start this conversation.

"Okay let me fill Key in. Look, when I was 16 Corey and I started messing around on the low. He was younger, so I didn't want to get him into any trouble plus with him being my brother's best friend, I didn't need any smoke with him. Once I became legal, he wanted to come out and tell Adonis and I didn't. Long story short, he found a new bitch and I found Malcolm. It was on some get back shit to be completely honest with you. I was mad that Adonis sent Corey away and even more made that Corey left. So, after dating Malcolm for only three months, he proposed and I accepted. He was the perfect distraction to what I was dealing with. Instead of telling my brother, I went to Vegas the next month and married Malcolm. It's one of my biggest regrets because I never loved him. I just finally wanted to do something that Adonis would not be able to control. I wanted to hurt him because I knew that he didn't want me marrying someone he hadn't approved of and that he would be hurt that he wasn't there for my big day. Although he didn't know how he hurt me or even that he hurt me, I still wanted to hurt him back.

I loved and still love Corey so much that the shit keeps me up at night. I'm married, and although I'm not happy I don't believe Malcolm deserves what I want to do to him. It's unfair that I played with his heart all those years ago and here I am again, ready to start a new game with him being on the losing end. Corey has been blowing me up since last night because he wants to see me and I'm not sure how much longer I can ignore him. My body craves him, my heart craves him, I crave him!" I finally released what I had been holding back.

"Damn, that's deep." Kewyn said. Again, we paused as our meals came out and she started again. "I mean, I see that you love Corey and that he loves you too. I understand that, but I see that this has the potential to get nasty also. You have to think of everyone involved, it's not just you. Think of how this will affect his relationship with your brother, your relationship with your brother, then there is Mika and of course Malcolm." She said making me think. Before I could say anything, Natasha did.

"Girl, fuck all of that. Malcolm is a big boy who will get over it. I'm sure Malcolm cares for you but his ass will find someone else, fall in love and have the family he cried about all the time. As for your brother, he only cares about himself anyway so he'll get over it. Baby, you can't hurt yourself worrying about other people. Go get your man!" Natasha said laughing. I noticed Kewyn rolling her eyes and knew they needed to stay far away from each other. Natasha couldn't fight but would pick until you just beat her ass. As for Kewyn, I could tell she was bout that life.

"I don't know, I'll decide soon. I have to anyway because he won't leave me alone." I replied, still confused.

"Sorry to cut this short but y'all were kind of late and my man is waiting on me. See you babe." Natasha said kissing my cheek but completely ignoring Kewyn's presence. I watched as Kewyn mugged her ass and she looked back at me.

"I don't like that bitch! And her cheap ass didn't pay for the food she barely touched." She said.

"You don't like her because of that Adonis comment." I said laughing.

"Nah, I don't like her because her ass seems sneaky and conniving. Watch your back because she didn't give a damn about what you had going on." She warned.

"Anyway, what was that with you and my brother?" I asked getting in her business.

"Man, I don't know. I was so sure that I wanted nothing more than to get out of here and go home but I was happy that I didn't make it to that plane. I was relieved on the cool. It's something about him that makes me want to dig deeper into his mind. I feel like I need to know more about him but it's so much that he doesn't know about me." She said.

"Look let me say this and then I'll mind my business for a while. Don't keep secrets from him because he will always find out the truth. When he loves, he loves hard but when he is through then he is through. My brother is everything you would want in a man but a lil crazier. Keep it real with him and never cross him!" I warned before the conversation switched up, I really hope that she was listening to me.

9

Corrupt

"Come here Mika." I saw she had a lil attitude and I wanted to ignore it, but I was really tripping lately. It was like, I couldn't focus on anything by Shy and the fact that she wasn't fucking with me. It had been two weeks since we all hung out at the club and since then her ass been making sure that she avoided me at all costs. She wasn't answering my calls or texts and I was tired of that shit.

"What you want Corrupt?" She asked walking over with an attitude.

"Where you going dressed like that? Your ass damn near hanging out them damn shorts. Why you got my shit on display?" I asked grabbing her by her ass and pulling her on my lap. She was straddling me, and my dick was reacting.

"Oh, you care? For the past few days your ass didn't give a fuck about anything I had going on, so I was going make another nigga happy." She said, rolling her eyes.

"Man chill out. I got some shit going on in the streets that have my full attention. I'm trying to work through some shit though so that we can get back right." I lied my ass off.

"You could have said that a long ass time ago Corrupt. Don't treat me like I'm the problem and have me sitting around wondering what I did wrong. I was racking my brains trying to see how could I fix some shit that I hadn't even broke. That's not fair to me. You know there ain't anything that I wouldn't do for you so all I ask is that you keep me in the loop. I thought you didn't want me anymore, man." A nigga felt a lil bad as I watched tears pool in her eyes. Using my fingers to wipe the tears, I wrapped my arms around her. I been fucking with Mika for going on a year and a half and she was solid. Her lil ass was fine as fuck and should be enough for a nigga. Her body was ridiculous, and she was drop dead gorgeous. I loved that she was feminine but not too soft. Being around Mika was easy, as long as Shay wasn't around. It would always come down to Shay, no matter who I was with. I was man enough to admit that, she had my heart and I didn't want it back.

"You tripping man. I love yo lil ass." I told Mika.

"So, I don't have anything to worry about?" She asked, pulling away and staring n my eyes.

"Nah. I'm fucking with you the long way." I replied. She leaned over and kissed my lips. Of course, I prolonged that shit. Gripping her hips, I moved them so that her pussy was grinding into my dick and just like that my man was waking up. I wanted some pussy so I hoped her ass wasn't in a rush because nothing was stopping me from fucking her silly.

"Noooo, I have to go meet Shay." As soon as she mentioned Shy, my dick went back to sleep. I didn't have the urge to fuck Mika no more cause she wasn't my Shy. "Sorry baby, she going squeeze me in right before her friend Natasha and I need a touch up." She said running her hands through her blonde extensions.

"You good. Tell Shy I said hit my line." I said tapping her thigh for her to get up.

"Why you call her that?" Mika asked.

"Her ass used to be hella shy around me." I said shrugging as if it was nothing.

"Oh, she doesn't strike me as the shy type." She said.

"You don't really know her. Let me know when you leave from the shop, so I can meet you here." I called out as she left out the house. I grabbed my phone and dialed Shy's number. Like I thought she would, her ass declined my fucking call. I was persistent as fuck though.

Me: Shy I ain't playing no more fucking games with you. If I ain't what you want, you gone have to tell me that in my face. Today, whether I have to show up at your house or you hit my line to come meet you somewhere. Just know, we are addressing this shit today.

I saw that she read the message but didn't respond. I would let her have that shit for now. Shy could play if she wanted to, but she knows a nigga ain't all there. I sat back in the chair and thought of the bullshit I was dealing with. Shy was a nigga's good thing and I was fucked up over her not being with me. You would think with all the time that had passed that I would be cool on her but that wasn't the case. Wasn't enough time left on Earth to fuck with the bond that we had created.

Shy was straight jail bait when I fell for her, but I couldn't help that shit. She went from being lil aggravating ass Shailen to damn that's Shailen, in the matter of a summer. I couldn't keep my eyes off of her and she was forever finding an excuse to come in my personal space. I used to find myself making excuses just to be in her presence because despite her age, her mind was full grown. She used to braid my hair and we would just run it. That shit all changed one day while Adonis was with some female. I had stopped by to kick it with him and he told me chill out cause, he knew I hated my home situation. Nigga said he would be a couple hours, so I went let Shy braid me up. When I went in her room, she was in the bathroom taking a shower, so I plopped in her bed and watched Tv. A glittery notebook caught my eyes, so I picked it up and opened the shit. As soon as I realized it was a diary, I went to close it but then I saw my name. Of course, that sparked my interest, so I sat there and read all of that shit. I didn't even notice that the shower wasn't on anymore until she walked out the bathroom all into her cell phone. She didn't notice me or I'm sure she would have run back into the bathroom. Her ass had strolled out as naked as the day she was born, and her body was that of a grown woman. Even back then I could tell that she wasn't about to be one of these skinny bitches. My Shy was stacked, and she didn't even know it. Reading her diary, I found out she had no confidence. She thought she was fat and thought that, that was the reason I didn't make a move on her.

"So, you want my attention but don't know how to say it huh?" I asked causing her to jump and drop her phone. When she noticed what I was reading, her mouth dropped. She didn't even realize she was naked.

"Corey, you can't read that!" She screamed.

"Why not? I like this part... I wish Corey knew how much I loved him. There were boys that tried to get with me, but I was saving myself for him. I didn't even..." I was reading from her diary when she jumped at me.

"Give it here!" She screamed as I lifted it higher, out of her reach. She was on her knees trying to catch the journal but her perky breast were in my face bouncing up and down. Before I could help it, I had my mouth filled with one. "Oh my God, Coreeeeeyyyy." She moaned out. I slid my fingers between her thighs and slid one along the outside of her pussy lips. That was enough to make her shudder. "Please." She begged.

"Please what Shy? What you want?" I asked. I noticed my dick was about to bust from my shorts.

"You! Corey, I don't want nobody but you!" As soon as she said that, her lips pressed into mine. When we were fucking was the only time Shy wasn't shy around me. That day, I became Shy's first. There wasn't a day that went by afterwards that we weren't fucking. We would be in the laundry room, the pantry, hell wherever we could be alone and not get caught, we were there.

I don't know how long I sat lost in my thoughts, but it had to be long because Mika texted me.

Mika: I'm done baby. Gonna stop and get some groceries so I can cook something special for you.

Me: Bet. I'm about to run out then I'll stop and get Shy to braid my shit.

Mika: You could have come with me.

Me: I had shit to do. I won't be long.

Mika: KK. Love you!

I didn't even answer her ass as I grabbed my keys and shot out. It was crystal clear that Shy forgot who the fuck I was. I was about to teach her though. I did the dash until I got to the house she shared with the fuck boy Malcolm. I saw her car parked out front but his wasn't. It could have been in the garage, but I really didn't give a fuck. Fuck him, I was here for his wife and my woman. Climbing the brick steps, I rang the doorbell while banging on the door. I heard footsteps coming to the door, but I still kept on banging. When the door swung open, Shay stood there with a gun in her hand and a mug on her face. When she realized it was me, there were a series of emotions displayed until they settled on fear.

"Are you crazy? You came to my house? What if my husband was here Corey?" She asked shooting out question after question.

"I am crazy, but you knew that. I told you contact me or I would come and fuck your husband. That nigga don't put fear in my heart." I replied.

"You have to leave!" She said.

"Nah, I'm going be wherever you at tonight." I responded pushing her in the house as I walked in. She tried to stop me but c'mon bruh. A nigga was 6'4 and pushing 289 pounds.

"What are you doing Corey!" She screamed still looking scared.

"Ma, I miss the fuck out of you." I said before her back hit the wall and I pulled her in for a kiss. Just like I knew, she didn't reject me. Her ass started kissing me back like she been waiting on me. I pulled the belt around her silk robe and was happy as fuck that she was completely naked underneath it. Without breaking our kiss, I plunged a finger into her pussy and that shit was leaking. Her juices was already dripping down my finger. I knew her ass was as ready as I was, so I pulled my shorts down just enough to release my dick.

"Wait, we can't do this. Not here baby." She moaned against my mouth.

"Man shut up, I'm getting in my pussy." I said before shoving my dick inside of her. Words failed her ass as she stared me in the eyes and if I didn't feel it a nigga saw all the love she had in her eyes for me. "This pussy still as tight as it was when I first slid in it. That nigga ain't fucking you right ma. You need to come back to daddy." I said as I hit her ass with some deep strokes.

"Corey... fuck.... Corey.... Ooooh fuck! I loveeeee you!" She screamed as she let her juices rain down on me. I was far from a minute man, but I couldn't hold back as a bust right behind her. I wasn't even started right so her ass was in trouble.

"I love yo ass too. Where is your room?" I asked picking her up.

"No, we can't baby please." She begged.

"Ma, I'm not finished with you." I said.

"But Mal..." she froze as we heard a noise.

"What's that?" I asked.

"The garage. Baby, go!" She cried out jumping down.

"Come with me." I said saving my dick.

"What you going do with Mika?" she asked.

"I'll hit your line. You better answer or I'm coming back and that nigga goin have to take the couch!" I said before kissing her and heading out the front door. The way their garage was positioned, it was no way he saw my car, but I really didn't give a fuck.

I IGNORED another call from Mika just as I heard the key card being slipped into the door. Throwing my phone down, I met Shy at the door and grabbed her bags.

"About time yo ass got here." I said pulling her further into the room. It was nothing for me to stand Mika ass up for Shy. The love we had was unmatched and the pussy was even better than I remembered.

"I had to get somethings from the store." She said.

"Like what?" I asked. She went into her bag and pulled out some magnums. I wasn't even tripping on using them cause, I was hitting Mika raw. I didn't want to disrespect Shy and earlier was reckless. "That's only one thing." I said.

"Oh, and this." She replied opening the coat she wore. Her ass was in a fucking school girl uniform. That was something I used to enjoy with her. Shy was a freak and loved role playing. I thought it was corny at first but with her, I loved it. I tried getting Mika to do it, but she didn't do the shit right. I was already butt ass naked and my dick ain't have time for that playing shit this go round though.

"We goin get back to that eventually. Right now, I'm trying to kiss all your sexy places." I said making her blush. Back when we were younger, and she was insecure, I would kiss all over her body to show where he sexy places were. I know that those insecurities were long gone thanks to me, but I never wanted them bitches to reappear. She thought her ass was leaving this room in the morning, but she was wrong. She was here for the weekend. We had lost times to make up for.

10

Kewyn

"What else you want to do today?" Adonis asked, with the smile on his face that I had grown to love.

"Oh my God, nothing! You have done so many things with and for me in this month that I don't think the city has anything left to offer." I said laughing. I thanked God daily for this nigga being crazy and kidnapping my ass before I got on that flight. This joy and happiness I felt since meeting him was unmatched. If this was some amazing once in a lifetime dream, then I prayed that I never woke up.

"You may be right. But then we can travel and do other shit." He said shrugging as if it was nothing. Hell, it was nothing to him.

"No silly. We can go to the super market later though. I don't want the chef to cook." I said. His eyes widened as we pulled up home.

"You cooking?" He asked.

"Nope, we cooking!" I said laughing. "We should invite everyone over too." I suggested.

"Whatever you want to do ma." He replied getting out of the car. I sat still because if I attempted to open that door he would want to kill my ass. As soon as he came around, he opened the door then leaned in and stole a kiss. That was the most we ever did, a lil kissing here and there but nothing too serious. Stepping out the car, I went around and helped him with all the bags that filled the trunk. It took both of us damn near three trips, but I couldn't really complain because about 75 percent of this shit was mine. As I saved both of our things where they belonged, my mind began to wonder. I wanted to go to work but he dismissed the fuck out of that idea. Then I had the idea to maybe go to school for real estate. I had been looking into it on Adonis' computer, but I wasn't sure just yet. Then in the back of my mind I couldn't help but to wonder what would happen to me when Adonis got tired of me. I was here with nothing but him and his family and friends but no one in my corner that wasn't directly connected to him. Shay and I were really cool but at the end of the day, she was his sister and not mine.

"What are you thinking about my pretty round brown." Adonis asked walking in and smacking me on the ass. I noticed he had a gift bag in his hand and wanted to know what that was about.

"Nothing and everything. What's that?" I asked nodding towards the bag.

"Mind your business, come here." He called me to where he was sitting on the bed and pulled me on his lap. "Tell me what's on your mind." He said.

"Well, I was really thinking about what I wanted to do next with my life. I don't want to just be here and not contribute anything to you or your household." I said.

"Didn't I tell you stop worrying about that shit." He said waving me off.

"Adonis, umm." I paused to find the words to say. "How long until Ty and Dez pay you back in full?" I asked. I noticed that his mood immediately changed.

"Why, you ready to dip?" He asked while laughing but I could tell it was a fake laugh. If I didn't know any better, I would say his feelings were hurt. He refused to look me in the eyes and his fists were balled.

"'It's not that at all. It's just that things have changed since I first came here. My feelings run deep, and I don't want to be thrown out like last week's trash once you get your money in your hand. I know that that's why you kept me around, but I fell for you and what it seemed like we were building. I didn't mean to because I knew that this was just business, but I couldn't help it. You are so easy to love, and you deserve that love. You are so caring and important to so many people that I felt it was my duty to care for you. And to make you the important person in the equation." I paused for a second and when he said nothing I felt like I needed to further explain myself. "Falling into a routine here, was easy. Too easy. I don't want to go back to Louisiana because there is nothing out there for me anymore. At the same time, I'm not trying to throw anything on you that you aren't ready for. I'm just worried about what happens to me, when it's all said and done." I finished. He was quiet for a while and I felt like shit. I decided to excuse myself but when I went to get up he stopped me.

"Where you going?" He asked.

"Find some pride." I damn near whispered as I fought for the tears to stay at bay.

"Yo ass bet not cry bruh. You had to give me time to find my words. I don't just blurt shit out." He said, and I felt a little relived. "I took so long to say something because I was honestly trying to calm the fuck down. You had me hot when your ass asked about that money. I thought you were ready to leave a nigga. I was hoping you never asked about that shit and we just kept rocking, if I'm being honest." He laughed.

"You want me to stay? Even after they pay you?" I asked feeling myself getting overly excited.

"Shit, they paid me last week. I just spent all that bread on you today." He said, and I quickly did the math. All we got was clothes and shoes. While it was high end shit, I just figured he had fronted them a crazy amount.

"You weren't going to say anything?" I asked, laughing and punching him in the arm.

"Say something for what? So, you could leave me? Nah shorty, I was going have your ass thinking they never paid me for years to come." He laughed.

"So that's all you want me for? A few years?" I joked.

"I want you for forever and a day." He replied without thinking. The way he stared in my eyes let me know he was dead ass serious.

"What are we doing here? Like you and I? What does this conversation change between us?" I asked.

"I'm goin keep it a stack and tell you that I love you and I think that I'm in love with you. The only reason I didn't make it official with you is because I feel like there is so much that we need to talk about. I know you hiding things from me but in the game I'm in, I don't have time for secrets." He said before grabbing the gift bag. "I got you somethings. Even before this conversation I wanted to show you that I was all in and that a nigga cared." He said handing it to me. I opened it and pulled out the first thing I touched.

"You brought me a Macbook?" I asked with my mouth wide open.

"Yeah, I know you like rose gold too, so I made that happen for ya. How else you going to real estate school without one?" He asked shocking me. "I'm very observant and I noticed you stayed checking that shit out on my laptop. Hopefully now you don't jack my shit no more." He added as he laughed. I couldn't join in on the laughter with him because I was too busy trying not to cry. "Yo ass bet not cry bruh." He said again. Digging in the bag again, I pulled out a yellow envelope. Breaking the seal, I pulled out banking info with both of our names on it. A card fell out that had my name on it too.

"Adonis, I don't want you for your money." I said shaking my head and handing him the envelope and its contents.

"Shit you ain't got access to it all no way." He said laughing. "But I don't ever want you to be without or feel you have to ask me for money whenever you want to do something. I told you I got you and that's my word. I know you been talking about a job so that you would have a safety net but know that if shit goes left, I'm going make sure you right. Here yo ass go. Give me my damn bag cause, I don't want yo cry baby ass to see the rest." He said trying to take my bag because I was crying.

"No, give me!" I said snatching it back. I dug to the bottom of the bag and all that was left was a small box. I grabbed it already knowing it was jewelry, but nothing prepared me for what was actually in it. I ripped off the top and froze when I saw a hey fob. "I know the fuck you didn't." I said jumping up and taking off down the stairs full speed. When I opened the door, I wanted to cry because I was so mad. I didn't ask for or need a car, but he didn't have to pull this prank. "I can't believe you did that to me. I was so excited." I literally stomped my feet and cried as I stared at the motorized toy Benz that was sitting next to his car. It was a beautiful plum color and that pissed me off even more.

"You mad at me ma?" He asked pulling me into his chest.

"Yeah. That was a tasteless joke Adonis." I said still crying until I heard Shay's voice behind me.

"I know I better be getting a new one real soon!" She called out as she pulled up behind the wheel of the full size benz. It looked just like the baby one in front of me. I couldn't help it as I jumped up and down all over again.

"Shay get out my shit!" I said running to it. Her ass hoped on the passenger side as I pulled off to drive her. "I can't believe this shit!" I kept saying over and over. Looking at Shay, I could tell her ass was happy for me but something else was on her mind. "What's wrong?" I asked her. She burst out crying and I pulled over to the side of the road. "What's wrong?" I repeated myself.

"I think that Malcolm is cheating on me." She said as if she couldn't breathe.

"Sorry, I have to ask. Why don't you use that as your excuse to leave? Then you can be with Corrupt like you really want to. I don't understand why you care." I said.

"I been with Corey for over a month now. I don't know how him and Mika even still maintain a relationship as much as we together." She said making my mouth fall open.

"First of all, how you crying over a nigga you cheating on? Second of all, bitch Malcolm ass cheated cause you stay with Corey somewhere fucking. What else he supposed to do?" I asked, rolling my eyes. Shay had to know that her ass was crazy as hell for this shit.

"I know, that's why I'm crying. Because I have to fall back from Corey so that I can catch Malcolm's ass in the act. After I fuck both of them up I'm going back to my man. I'm not crying over Malcolm. I'm crying because dick too bomb to go weeks without it." She said with big tears falling from her eyes. Hell naw, let me get this bitch out my car. Driving back home, my phone started ringing and I was shocked that Dez's name flashed across my screen. I hadn't talked to her ass since I told her off and I honestly was curious to know why she called. I knew I couldn't answer now so I was even quicker to get back home.

11

D^{ez} After calling Kewyn a sixth time I was ready to give up, but something told me to try just one more time.

"What Dez, fuck!" She snapped answering on the first ring.

"Kewyn, you don't think that it's past time that we talked?" I asked forgetting the real reason I was calling. She seemed so much more important.

"Nope. We have nothing to talk about. Say what you have to say so that I can get back to my man." She said shocking me.

"Your man?" I asked getting pissed off. "What fucking man? Is Ty there?" I asked.

"Hell motherfucking no. Ty is nobody's man baby. He was just a grown ass boy!" She replied.

"So, he hasn't contacted you?" I asked.

"Dez, I haven't heard from him since y'all sold me out. From the bottom of my heart, fuck you and Ty!" She replied before ending the call. I wanted to call her back and make her hear me out, but I couldn't. I had more important things to tend to. Like this body on the floor. When I killed the bitch, I wasn't fully aware of who she was and now I didn't know what the fuck this would do to my man.

"Stupid bitch!" I said kicking the body. "Why the fuck did you have to fuck shit up?" I said pacing around the body. I don't see how I didn't see the resemblance before, but Felisha looked just like her brother, Jason. When I heard banging on the door I took a deep breath and said a prayer. I hope this didn't fuck with him too much, but I did what I had to do. The bitch knew too much, and it was his fault. I swung the door open and my pussy throbbed at the sight of him.

"Where she at?" He asked. I stepped back and let him in the house. He walked into the front room and I watched pain reflect across his face. "Fuck man! Fuck!" He said punching the air.

"Baby, I didn't know." I explained.

"Nah man, this one is on me. I should have seen this shit. What happened?" He asked and even though I already told him, I started from the start.

"Earlier when you came to the shop, her ass ducked out. I didn't realize it because I was too busy focusing on you. Anyway, after you left I went look for her because her phone was ringing but when I looked down it was Ty's picture on the phone. So, I went to the bathroom and looked through her texts and she had been feeding him information. The last text message she sent to him was that you were out, and we were working together. He told her he would get low and contact her later. I powered the phone off and took it with me home. I turned it on once I got here and she kept calling from the shops phone. I lied and told her I accidently took it and she could come pick it up any time. Her ass flew here, and I invited her in. She saw the pictures of me, Ty and Kewyn and started asking questions. I could tell she was getting mad, so I excused myself. I was ear hustling at the door when she called him and started going off about how happy we looked and how hurt she was. He must have hung up on her, so I came out with my gun and confronted her. She refused to give him up. Told me she hoped he killed you and I because we were trying to come between their love. Her love for him made her hate you. When I told her that you were going to kill him, she charged me. We got to fighting and the gun went off. With her last breath she still called out for Ty. I went through her phone. When I started working at the shop is when they crossed paths. Every time she went to visit you was because he sent her for information. She was pregnant." I finished. I jumped as he punched a hole in the wall.

"That nigga has no more times to try me! He is dying real fucking slow when I get my hands on his bitch ass!" He roared. "Burn this shit down and let's go!" He demanded before walking out. I was actually sad to burn it down because we had only been in here for a couple weeks. Ty knew we couldn't stay in an apartment complex and the plan was to move and bring Kewyn back. Once a lil power got to Ty's head, he switched up. He didn't want Kewyn anymore. I didn't think on it for much longer before I went to the shed and grabbed the gas can. I threw gas everywhere before throwing a match and hauling ass. Climbing in the car with Jason, I reached over and tongued him down. This was my nigga without the title because we had a sick bond. From the jump it had always been he and I.

You see, when I would be going visit my man in jail, I was visiting Jason. He was in jail for the same lick that Ty was in jail for. They were actually caught together but Ty's ass turned snitch. Ty didn't know me because I wasn't Jason's woman. We were fuck buddies but when he got popped, I stepped up as his ride or die. I was there weekly, smuggling any drug you could name in through my pussy. Then a guard that he was breaking off told him about Ty turning informant against him and we started a plan for revenge. The day I met Kewyn was pure coincidence. I was always attracted to women so when I saw her fine ass stranded at the bus station in the rain, I offered her the ride. Jason knew I was bisexual, so it was nothing for me to tell him about the bad lil broad I had befriended. He immediately knew who she was, I mean her name itself was a giveaway. It was then that our plan came together. I was to get close to this nigga so that I was able to take him out. Then, I took it a step further. I decided my man deserved to come out on top when it was said and done. When Adonis came in to cut his hair, I put my persuasive skills to use.

It took no time to get him to agree to a sit down but that didn't go well until Kewyn showed up. It was fucked up how I pawned her off, but I had my reasons. I didn't mean to fall in love with her, but I did. Sending her away ensured that she was safe while we got rid of Ty. After we got rid of the first product and re-upped, I faked like we were robbed and used that money to get my man a bomb ass lawyer who had the case dismissed. Kewyn was still a big factor though, I planned on going get her when it was all said and done and then maybe we could replace Ty with Jason. I never planned on her falling for someone else. I didn't give up easily though. Once we were done with Ty, I was going get her ass.

12

Kewyn

"Movvvvvveeeee baby!" I said swatting Adonis away from me as he kissed on my face. I was trying to sleep but he was being annoying.

"Nah, get yo ass up. We have shit to do." He said slapping my ass. All the fuck he did was play with my ass all damn day. His ass was obsessed or something.

"What do I have to do? I don't start school until next week. I just want to sleep." I whined.

"So, you not getting up?" He asked?

"Nooooo!" I screamed. He laughed but I heard him walk out the door and listened to him head down the stairs. Turning over, I got comfortable again and started to drift back into sleep. What felt like seconds later, I woke up ready to swing on Adonis because he flipped the covers off and slapped fire from my ass. Jumping up, I was shocked because it wasn't him.

"That's why he kidnapped your ass. That booty do be moving boo." Adonis' mom said laughing. Y'all this bitch was bad! Like its no way in hell that she had two grown ass children. She looked young as hell and I could tell she didn't have a lick of makeup on. On top of that, she was fine as hell. Her waist line was missing but her ass and hips sure the fuck wasn't.

"Girl, I almost slid your ass. I thought you were Adonis fucking with me again." I said rolling my eyes. My ass was stinging so I rubbed it. "I didn't know you were back in town." I added. We had spoken a few times on facetime, so she wasn't completely a stranger to me.

"I'm back for a few days and then I'm leaving again. Shay and Adonis both know that it is very rare for me to sit around. I raised and spoiled their asses so now it's time for them to spoil me. Get up and get dressed, I'm cooking." She said walking out of the room and closing the door behind her. I couldn't help but laugh as I dragged my feet to the shower. Although I really wanted to get some sleep in, I was excited to spend time with Sierra. I took a quick shower, brushed my teeth and went to slip on some clothes. Picking up my phone, I noticed in the short amount of time I was in the bathroom, I had ten missed calls from an unsaved number. Clicking on the number, I called it back and listened as it rang. When the call was answered, I was greeted with silence.

"Hell, is anyone there?" I called out. I listened a lil longer but there was no answer. "Umm, hello?" I repeated myself. Still, nothing. Just as I was going to hang up, they spoke.

"Kewyn, please don't hang up." I heard Ty's voice and honestly felt nothing. I didn't miss him nor was I filled with rage anymore. I just didn't care. Because of what he and Dez did, I was happier than ever.

"Hey Ty. Dez called looking for you, you should call your girl back because I'm a little busy." I nonchalantly responded.

"Man, fuck Dez! If that bitch calls you back, don't fucking answer." He demanded like he ran something over here.

"I can do you one better, I won't answer for either of you. I don't know what's going on with the two of you, but I really don't want to be involved. Enjoy your life." I said going to hang up the phone. Before I could remove it from my ear he started talking again.

"Kewyn man, wait fuck! I don't know what got into your ass, but I need you. That's the only reason I'm calling you. Dez ain't who we thought she was her ass used you to get close to me. She was working with Jason." He said pissing me off.

"Nigga, what do you mean what got into me? Need I remind you what the fuck you did to me? You threw me in another nigga's arms like I meant nothing to you. Fuck you and Dez! I don't give a fuck who she really is because at this point that's your problem. I'm only worried about me and Adonis." I snapped.

"Adonis? Don? So what, you fucking that nigga Don now?" He asked.

"Yes, Adonis is my man now. Thanks to you and Dez. So as you can see, I'm not tripping on y'all no more. I even did y'all a solid and paid off my car. Y'all can keep it as a parting gift." I replied with a shrug.

"Man look, Dez and Jason were setting me up! They want me dead and are stopping at nothing to see it happen. I drove way out here thinking you were going to skip town with me because I'm sure they will hurt you too. They robbed me, and I don't have shit to my name Kewyn." He said tugging at my heart strings. No matter how much I didn't want him, I didn't want him to end up dead.

"I- I don't know what you want me to do Ty." I said.

"You know I don't have anyone else ma. If I did, I wouldn't even bother you. I need some bread. Just enough for me to disappear. I'm about to text you the address to this park. I'll be there in about an hour, please come through for me Kewyn. You invited Dez into our situation, this wouldn't have even happened. I'll be waiting." He said hanging up the phone. Sitting on the bed, I took a deep breath and said a prayer. I knew without a doubt that I would help him, but I didn't want this to back fire on me. I slid on a matching bra and panty set before heading to the closet and grabbing a bright orange crop top sweater with the matching sweat pants and the new rainbow colored Air Max I had. Before walking out, I went into the safe and grabbed a few stacks of money. After quickly dressing and throwing the money in a Louis Vuitton back pack purse, I went downstairs.

"Your ass sure came down quick for her huh?" Adonis teased.

"Shut up, you could have simply said she was here." I said laughing and taking a seat at the island. Adonis got up from his seat and made his way over to me.

"I don't get a kiss?" He asked, making me blush. Even after he and I spoke, I wasn't one hundred percent sure where we stood. It's not like he came out and asked me to be his woman, so we still hadn't had sex. His kisses always left me wanting more though so I didn't want his mom to see that.

"But your mom is right there." I whisper motioning towards Sierra who was at the stove.

"Kewyn, I'm a grown ass man in my own house. I said give me a kiss." He demanded. That shit was hella sexy and I'm sure the look on my face showed because he started rubbing the back of his head and biting his lip. I laughed when he grabbed his dick and motioned up the stairs with his head. I silently shook my head with a huge smile on my face as I made sure his mom's back was still to us.

"Y'all obvious as fuck." She said not looking back. My mouth fell open, but Adonis' ass bust out laughing. "How y'all went from talking about a kiss to being quiet. I hear your damn earrings jingling so you shook your head at something. Y'all probably being nasty and I ain't mad at y'all because once I leave here, I'm going get it in too." She said throwing one hand in the air and popping her ass with her tongue hanging out her mouth.

"Yeah, alright. Get you and that fuck nigga fucked up." Adonis said mugging her. I didn't hear her response because my phone went off alerting me of the text that just came in. Opening it, I noticed the address Ty sent was about twenty minutes away from here. I was supposed to meet him in thirty minutes. I wanted to tell Adonis that my "brother" needed help but then Adonis would want to come along to make sure his product wasn't fucked with. Come to think about it, he may flat out say hell no at letting him get more money out of him. It wasn't a secret that he thought my "brother" was on some other shit for offering me up. He made it crystal clear that he did not trust or fuck with Ty. So, as much as I didn't want to, my only option was to add this to the other secret I kept tucked away. Again, I prayed that it didn't come back to bit me in my ass.

"Huh?" I jumped when Adonis tapped me.

"Damn, you were staring off and damn near chewing your lip off. Ma was having a whole conversation with your ass and you didn't hear shit. You ok?" Adonis asked.

"Yeah, thinking about my brother." I didn't really lie. He did know Ty as my brother.

"Oh, he good?" He asked.

"Yeah, I just have to send off some paperwork I have for him before it's too late. I'm about to run out and handle that. I'll be right back though." I lied. Adonis didn't seem to notice.

"Your ass just wants to drive that car. Be careful ma." He said kissing my lips like he wanted too anyway. Just like always, I never wanted it to end but I pulled away anyway. Looking at the Rolex he got me to match one of his many, I knew it was time to go.

"Be right back!" I called out and jumped in my car. Turning on the gps, I smoothly made it to the park and pulled into a parking spot far in the back. I didn't know many people, but I didn't need for any of Adonis' workers to see me with Ty. Adonis would want to know why was he in town and I kept that away from him. While waiting, I opened my kindle app and started reading this book titled, Tampering with a Thug's heart by Coco Shawnde. Baby girl was wicked with a pen and I enjoyed all of her series. I was so engrossed in the story that I didn't realize, Ty was here until he knocked on the window. With my hand on my chest I lowered it.

"You scared me." I said.

"Should have been paying attention to your surroundings. I just told you that niggas was after me so you need to be alert." He warned.

"I have nothing to do with you, so they aren't after me." I replied.

"You a part of me ma, they'll gun for you just to get to me." My eyes shot up when he said that.

"No Ty, I was a part of you. I'm not anymore and Adonis can protect me." I saw anger flash in his eyes briefly. I could understand him being mad though. Shit wasn't supposed to happen like this.

Since we were younger, it was supposed to be he and I against the world. Shit happens, and people change though.

"Damn ma, that shit hurt a nigga in the heart." He said. I slowly opened the door and stepped out of my car. Closing the door back, I leaned against it as we just stared at each other for a few minutes. He was staring at me like he was trying to fight the urge to kiss me and I was staring at him trying to see if I felt anything for him anymore. I didn't. That shocked me, because although I wanted out a long time ago I just couldn't leave. I'm not sure if love made me stay or if loyalty did. "What happened to us?" He asked as if he read my mind.

"Life. We were both set on survival when we met as teens. That shit bonded us into our adult hood. But when you know better, you want better and that makes you do better. While we were living in our first rat infested spot, I watched people happily living their lives and I wanted that. They weren't relying on stealing and maybe selling enough weed to eat. So, while you were happy that we were just together, I wasn't. Then I got a job, and we weren't together as often. I felt our bond getting a little loose then, but I didn't say anything because I didn't think it was a big deal. Me working gave me a little hope but you pulled back from me. You started hugging the block tighter than you were hugging me. It's like you wanted to be in a competition and I wasn't on that shit. I was trying to come up for us, but your ego felt threatened. That didn't help get us right, then boom you went to jail. We were already in a bad space all because you were being selfish. How many times had I told you that I could get you on in the hospital's kitchen or as a maintenance man?" I asked.

"Man, I wasn't built to do that shit." He replied, showing me he still hadn't grown from way back then.

"But you were built to be in jail? Dumbest shit I ever heard. Anyway, our shit was already rocky and Dez filled that void. So, when you said earlier that I brought Dez in our life, you were wrong. You did. Had you been at home with me and not in the streets with Jason, you wouldn't have gotten locked up. I wouldn't have been at visitation. And I would have never met Dez. Not to mention, my loyalty to you left the building when you sold me to the highest bidder. Everything in life happens for a reason." I finished.

"And what was the reason of all this shit?" He asked, looking frustrated.

"It was to give me my out. I was ready to leave but I was holding myself back for all the wrong reasons. In that whole equation, I was the only one making sacrifices. I don't know if I would have ever left if you had not damn near kicked me out. So now that you have figured out Dez was working with the enemy, what now?" I asked, genuinely concerned. I didn't want him, but I didn't want him hurt either.

"I take the money you giving me and I get low. I have to kill Jason because if not, he goin kill me. I just need them to think shit sweet for a while." He said. Ty wasn't a killer, in fact I think he was coward. But you know a coward will shoot quicker than anyone else. "You know you can come, right?" He asked.

"No, no I can't. My life is here now, what we had was in that past. I will always have love for you and you are still a part of my prayers. But our book has ended." I said with no hesitation. I meant every word that flowed from my lips.

"Bet. So what, I can't call you from time to time?" He asked looking a little desperate. You know that all I have in this world is you, man. Don't cut me off like that." He begged.

"Yeah, you can." I replied lying through my teeth. As soon as he left town, I would be changing my number. I felt sorry for him, but I couldn't drag him into my new relationship. Ty was handsome, he would meet another woman.

"Cool." He said looking relived. "You got that money?" He asked. Nodding my head, I bent over into the car to grab my bag and I felt his arms around my waist. "Let me hit it for old time's sake." He said as his fingers rubbed my pussy through the sweatpants. My eyes rolled into my head because it had been too damn long since I got dick. I felt his poking me in the ass and his hands slid into the front of my pants and found my pussy. With his fingers, he started making love to my clit for about five second until I grabbed his wrist. Snatching it from my pants, I turned around with the book sack purse in my hand. He was still right in my face and I was panting hard as hell. I wanted it so damn bad but not from him. His dick was poking me, so I softly pushed him back.

"All I have left for you is this money, please don't do that again." I said digging in my bag and handing him the cash.

"Damn, you really ain't fucking with a nigga. How much is that?" He asked.

"Does it fucking matter? It's more than you had to begin with, right? Take it and stay safe." I quickly said before hopping in my car and speeding off. My heart was racing, my panties were wet, but I felt a sense of relief. Ty was in my past and there was no room for him in my future.

"MY MAMA ENJOYED SPENDING time with you today." Adonis said, as I lay with my back on his chest in his huge bathtub.

"Really? She told you that?" I asked.

"Nah, she didn't have to though, I could tell. Her ass don't ever stay around my house all damn day. She has a one hour limit with me. Her and Shay barely do ten minutes in each other's presence alone. They always at each other's neck so I know she enjoyed bonding with you." He said making me smile.

"I really enjoyed talking with her also. I've never been able to do that because my mom loved men more than she loved me. She was always gone, and I was always home. At first, she would send me money to get food and school shit but after a while, nothing. The calls stopped, her popping in for a day or two stopped and before I knew it, I hadn't saw her in like four months. She wouldn't take my calls and after a while changed her number. Then the eviction notice came. I wa- I was fifteen. I was just fifteen, Adonis. She left me alone and never looked back. What did I do that was so damn wrong? I never got in trouble, I made good grades and I didn't talk back. Why couldn't she love me?" I cried. I felt him slightly lifting me from the water and turning me so that I was now facing him. I tried hiding my face because I knew I was doing the ugly cry, but he wouldn't let me.

"Baby, sometimes people can only love you the way they were loved. They can't pull love from the sky because love can't be taught. It's something you feel over time. If she never felt love, then she didn't know how to give love. I'm not making an excuse for her, but look at you. You are a survivor, a nigga would never have known you went through shit like that from looking at you. Fuck the love you didn't get back then, I'm going love you until it hurts. Our future children going love you and they nappy head ass children, goin love you too." He said making me laugh.

"Children?" I asked.

"Yeah, I want like seven of them running around this bitch!" He said smiling and nodding his head.

"I ain't pushing out seven kids Adonis." I said laughing.

"Shit yeah you are! As soon as I throw a ring on that finger, we starting." He said pulling my lips into his. This kiss, like all the others was amazing. I'm sure my pussy got so wet that the damn water in the tub would overflow. When he pulled back, I wanted to cry. "I don't have no secret kids, no crazy ex's, I caught too many bodies to count, I'm still in the game but my hands no longer get dirty, and you will always be protected."

"Huh?" I asked, confused.

"I needed you to open up before I made us official and I wanted to make sure you knew what you were dealing with." He said as I smiled. "You good with that?" He asked, and I nodded. "Anything I need to know?"

"I have no secrets." I lied and kissed his lips again. I felt his dick growing and I began rubbing my pussy against it. We bathe and slept together so it wasn't like I was new to it, the bitch was just big as fuck. All those nights it lay behind me, it was never hard. Well, it was hard but it wasn't against me. He was very respectful about it. On today, I knew that we weren't just going to ignore it. He slightly lifted me up once more, before placing his dick at my entrance.

"Look ma, I'm going do all kinds of romantic and nasty shit to you and your pussy once we get out of this tub. But for right now, I just need to feel you and get you ready for later." He warned looking me in my eyes.

"Please, be gentle." I wouldn't say don't hurt me because I knew there would be some pain. But I also knew, the pleasure wasn't going to be too far behind.

"I will, while we in this tub. No promises after we get out." He said before sliding me down his dick. As my pussy stretched around it, the only thing I heard was the curse words he was moaning. As for me, I'm sure I looked like a blow up doll. My mouth. And eyes were wide open, and I wasn't even halfway on the dick. It was so fat and long that I wasn't sure it would even fit! Adonis grabbed my hips and slid me up and down the part he did work in. After a while, the pain passed and I was grabbing at my weave trying to contain myself.

"Fuck baby, fuck!" I said. This shit was driving me wild and the fact that he was staring me directly in my eyes while biting his bottom lip didn't help. Moving his hands, I firmly placed my feet in the tub and lowered myself further down his dick. The pain was nothing compared to the pleasure I was experiencing. "Oh fuck, I'm about to cummmmm." I said as I felt my juices squirt from my pussy and mix with the water. With the extra help from my juices, I slipped right onto his lap. My pussy and stomach was, filled with rock hard, grade A dick and I wouldn't have it any other way.

"God damn, that pussy squeezing the fuck out my dick." He moaned as he moved his lips below me. "I can barely move in this shit." He said with his face frowned up. Deciding to help him, I went right back to bouncing on his dick as he held my ass cheeks.

"Was it worth the wait bae?" I asked wrapping my arms around his neck.

"Hell naw, if I knew it was this good you wouldn't have made it the first night you got here." He replied slowly making love to my pussy. I felt myself about to nut again and he must have known he was hitting my spot because he stared in my eyes again and started pounding it. Gone were those long deep strokes, he was now on attack mode and I swear to God my eyes were looking at my brain. I couldn't even cry out, I was so completely fucked up over what he was doing to my body. My leg got stiff and then started shaking as I rained down on his dick once more. Pulling me off his dick, this nigga raised me in the air like I was nothing and put my pussy in his mouth. With my legs wrapped around his head, I grinded my pussy harder and harder until he was quenching his thirst. I was dead ass listening to him gulp as he feasted on my goods. I was too weak for words and just wanted sleep, but he wasn't done with me. Instead of placing me back in the tub he slightly turned my body and his tongue went into my ass. I had done some things with Ty and Dez but I ain't never got licked from my pussy to my asshole. The feeling was out of this world and though I was enjoying it, it made me want the dick even more. Bringing my fingers to my pussy, I started finger fucking myself until he came up for air.

"Don't fucking touch my pussy. From this day forward, you only touch my pussy when I say to. And I won't ever say no lame shit like that. You feeling nasty, come be nasty on this!" He said before sitting me back on his hard dick. "You hear me Kewyn. This my pussy. A nigga bet not think about my pussy or I'm killing his ass!" He roared as he filled me up with his seeds. I fell onto his chest to catch my breath, but he wasn't having it. With his semi erect dick still in me, he lifted us up and walked us over to the shower. With each step, his dick got harder and harder. By the time he had us under the warm stream of water, he had me screaming and nutting all over his dick. I could tell I would need a damn cane to walk playing with his ass.

13

Corrupt

I sat on the chair in the corner of the room scrolling through my phone. I wasn't really look for or at shit, I was just trying to keep myself busy. Looking at the box that set on my lap, I shook my head. This ring set a nigga back a bit, but if anyone else was worth it Shy was. It fucked with me that she had been ignoring me, but I think I knew why. Shy saw Mika in the picture and felt like I was playing games with her. She was worried about Mika not knowing that Mika was living on her time. Only reason Mika was still around is because Shy was playing games. For a few weeks we would be locked up in this very room damn near every night, fucking in every inch of it. When we weren't fucking we were just doing us. Talking, eating, watching movies, making movies, whatever she wanted to do, I was doing. But I wasn't about to keep our relationship hidden behind these doors. I wasn't that lil nigga anymore. Shy had to know that us being hidden was a thing of the past. Tonight, she needed to let me know if I was wasting my time or not. I saw it in Mika's eyes and the way she acted that she was tired of the sun beating me home. I noticed her ass had slowly started packing her things into some luggage and pushing it in the corner of the closet. I was an observant nigga, but I played like I had no clue. Depending on how tonight went, determined if I was making her unpack or helping her pack the rest. When the door opened, I hid the ring in the cushion of the chair.

"Was that really necessary?" Shy asked walking in the room. I couldn't even focus on the look on her face because she was wearing another one of those trench coats. Anytime she showed up to this room, it was always something sexier than the previous selection hidden beneath it. My mind was on what could it have been today. "Corey, you are going too far. Why would you do that shit?" She asked, and I shrugged at her ass.

"Because I can! Shy you are for me, not that nigga! Fuck him! You in your feelings because I was in your crib, fuck that house. That should have been our house! You mad cause a nigga was ass naked in the bed waiting on you? If that was our shit, you would have to get used to is because that's how I was waiting every damn day!" I spat.

"But Corey, what if he would have gotten home before me? You were in bed beating your dick like I don't have a husband." She said not knowing that shit was falling on deaf ears.

"If he would have gotten there before you, I would have beat his ass for seeing my dick. No nigga going look at my dick and get away with it." I replied. "You acting mad now, but what you did when you saw me? You didn't say get out, you didn't check on your husband. Your ass licked your lips and asked why was I there, right?" I asked standing up and walking over to her. Her breathing got slower as I grabbed her by the belt of her coat and ripped it off. She was in some all white lingerie and all I could picture is what our wedding night would be like. "Right, Shy?" I asked again.

"Mhmm." She answered as I slid my hand into the crouchless panties and stroked her pussy.

"I can't hear you. What did you do?" I asked.

"I li-licked my lips and I sa-said I missed you but wh- why were you in my house." She said shuddering at my touch. Dropping my jeans and my boxers, I stepped out of them and kicking them out of my way. I grabbed her hand and placed it on my dick.

"And then I said what?" I asked as she started stroking it.

"You said you were there for your woman and your pussy." She repeated my words.

"And then you walked to the bed, got naked and you said?" I urged her to continue as I turned her around, so she was facing the door and her ass was to me.

"If this was your pussy, what are you waiting on to take it?" As soon as she finished her sentence I plunged my dick deep into her guts. I bent her forward from her waist and started fucking her like my life depended on it. Gripping her hips, her pussy immediately started convulsing around my dick. I knew she was about to nut, so I pulled out of her. "Corrreeeeyyyyyy." She whined.

"Lay on the bed." I demanded. She damn near ran to the bed and laid on her back. I pulled her legs so that her ass was hanging off the edge and shoved my dick back into her while massaging her clit with my thumb. As soon as I felt her convulsing again, I stopped. I didn't pull my dick out of her though. Her eyes shot open and I would be dead if looks could kill. "Ma, I got the pussy, but I still left without my woman. As much as I enjoyed that shit, I was still cheated out of why I was really there. I'm ready for it to be just us two. No more hiding, no more rooms. I want every fucking body to know that Shay belongs to Corrupt and Corrupt belongs to Shay." I said as I started fucking her again. My strokes were deep and sensual, and I could tell she was going crazy. Then I stopped.

"Corrreeeeyyyy!" She whined again.

"Say something Shy, please?" I was begging her ass and I didn't have any shame. Shy was the only woman I ever truly loved, and I was willing to risk the friendship I built with her brother for it. It wasn't just a friendship I could lose. I was eating with that nigga. No nigga could make me starve but he could make it real hard for me to keep my pantry filled.

"What you want me to say Corey?" She asked, pissing me off. Grabbing her waist, I started pounding into her.

"Fucking say you going leave that nigga. Give him his fucking walking papers and be with me. You say you love me, often! So, either you lying or you were waiting for this invitation. Be with a nigga man.

Marry me!" I roared pulling out of her again because now I was about to bust.

"What about Mika?" She asked.

"You got my dick chilling in your guts with your juices leaking from it on Mika's birthday. A nigga begging you to be with me, on Mika's birthday. A nigga saying marry me, on Mika's birthday. Man, fuck Mika!" I spat.

"I need a little more time." She said. Without another word, I took my frustrations out on her pussy. This wasn't even for her at this point, this was for me. "Wait baby, slow down." She called out, but it was too late. I pulled my dick out of her and my nut slowly leaked out too.

"Time's up Shy." I said grabbing my clothes and walking into the bathroom. I cleaned off my dick and got dressed before walking out and her ass was sitting up in the bed staring at me.

"Where are you going? You aren't spending the night? I made plans to stay." She said. I chuckled and shook my head.

"You can stay, leave your card on the bed cause I'm going take my card off file in the morning." I said walking to the chair to grab the ring.

"Why? I like this hotel." She stated.

"You not getting it huh? It's no more of this Shy and Corey game you like to play. A nigga too fucking old to be sneaking around and dicking down another nigga's bitch!" I spat. "You love your husband so much that you can't fucking leave that miserable ass shit and be with the nigga you supposedly love? The nigga who loved you since forever bruh?" I asked touching the tattoo at the temple of my head. Timod'samor was written in a real close script as one word, if anyone would have looked that shit up they would know it said Shy's love. "If you love that nigga so fucking much, you need to stay off my dick and hop on his shit." I spat grabbing my shit through my jeans.

"Corey, I just asked for some fucking time!" She screamed with tears in her eyes. That shit wasn't moving me tonight.

"Your ass been asking for time since you were eighteen Shailen. I'm all out of time ma." I shrugged and went to walk out.

"This is an excuse ain't it? You needed an excuse to leave and go back to the bitch, Mika and this is the one you chose. Nigga you ain't have to play this lil game tonight. You could have simply said that you had shit to do. You'll be back and I'll think about answering your calls." She spat, pissing me off.

"My calls? Ma, its nothing with you and me no more. A nigga name ain't got to ever running across your screen anymore. Matter of fact, I guarantee it won't. I'm a grown ass man and you talking about games? I just asked you to marry me and your ass still screaming time! This look like a fucking game?" I asked opening the ring box. I was all in, you fucked this up."

"Wait, I didn't know you were serious." She said with her eyes wide open.

"I been serious, you just never took me serious. Whole time I was entertaining your ass and I had a rider in my corner. I'm running behind you trying to convince you that I'm the nigga for you, but that shit was a lie. You got your nigga, this was fun but I'm going get my woman." I said before closing the box and storming out. I heard her screaming my name but fuck Shy.

14

Shay

I felt my heart literally break into pieces as Corey walked out on me. I never wanted to hurt him, but I was blinded by revenge. He wouldn't even let me explain. I guess he thought I would choose Malcolm over him, but I wouldn't I would give up everything for him. I just couldn't get pass the words he said. Was I really a waste of time to him? Did he really regret what we had? How can you say you love someone and then hurt them so bad? Dragging myself out the room, I hoped in my car and blindly drove home in silence. Jesus had to be with me because I cried the whole way home in a daze. That tone of his voice was so final. Like there was no coming back from what he said. I knew he meant that shit by the look in his eyes. I was happy that Malcolm wasn't here because I didn't have the energy to fake anything. I was hurting, and it was clear to see. This shit felt like the first time he left all over again, just worse. They lied when they said the first cut was the deepest, because this one went way deeper.

Stopping in the kitchen, I opened my wine cellar and grabbed a bottle. I didn't even know what brand it was. I just knew that I needed this shit. I clicked the lights back off and left. Walking to my bedroom felt like it took forever. I didn't want to go back in that damn room. It reminded me of the fact that I was really on the wrong side of the perfect love story. The closer I walked towards that room, the harder it got to breath. Corey was supposed to be my forever but now Mika got to luck up on my fuck up. I hooked my phone up to my beats pill and went to the song I listened to over and over the first time he left. Stripping naked, I sat in the middle of the bed and drunk my wine straight from the bottle as I ruined Monica's song. The first time I heard this song it hit me in the heart so hard, and even that had nothing on how I felt singing it now.

Boy it's been a long time since the last time I saw you. Feels like nothing changed since we been together, I must admit that I feel crazy about you. And I can see it in your eyes that there something you want to say to me. Cause usually right now you would be holding onto me! But instead you're telling me that things have changes they're not the same. That recently you found someone that you decided to dedicate your whole life to, and what we had has to be through. And baby what hurts the most is letting go, I just want you to know that I love so. And I know things are different now, you've gone and settled down. I thought for sure you'd always wait for me, I tell you what hurts the most. Is that should have took the chance, boy when you came to me and offered me your hand. Silly of me I thought I would always have your heart; I had the chance to have all your love. Oh, how I'm missing you now.

After a whole bottle of wine and listening to the song on repeat at least ten times, it was safe to say I was a lil past drunk. I was over the song, so I pressed shuffle and Lord why did I do that? Her Room, Teyana Taylor's version of Marvin's Room came on and it put me in a completely different mood. My sadness turned into a blind rage. If I was honest with myself, the truth was I had no one to blame but myself. But fuck it, I wasn't being honest. I grabbed my phone and called Corey. After two rings, his ass ignored my call, so I kept trying until he answered. I must have been on the seventh call before he answered.

"Shailen, chill with this shit." Nothing hurt me as much as that little sentence.

"Sha- Shailen? Did you just call me Shailen?" I asked. It felt like my heart paused while we waited for his answer.

"Ain't that your name shawty?" He spat back.

"Not to you! I'm Shy! Call me Shy!" I damn near pleaded as tears fell from my eyes.

"Where you at man, you sound like you been drinking." He said after releasing a deep sigh. I could picture him running his hand down his face and felt myself smiling. I always knew just how to frustrate my baby.

"I just, I just need you to call me Shy and tell me you love me again. Tell me that you only said those things because you were angry and that you're sorry." I pleaded.

"Shailen, where you at man?" He asked again.

"CALL ME SHY! MY NAME IS SHY!" I snapped. I almost fell over as I stood from the bed still clutching the empty bottle of wine. "Don't fucking call me that, ok baby? I just need to hear you say you love me again Corey. Do you still love me?" I asked crying.

"I thought I did. I'm not so sure anymore." He said. If it felt like he stabbed me earlier, then this felt like him pulling the knife out.

"What? You- you don't love me anymore? You don't mean that baby. I fucked up, I know I fucked up, but I can fix this. We can fix this." I said pleading for him to agree with me. "Can't we fix this, Corey?"

"Ma, our ship has sailed. Sleep that liquor off, I'm goin hang up before Mik.." He started.

"DON'T YOU DARE MENTION THAT BITCH'S NAME COREY!" I screamed throwing the wine bottle into the mirror that was above our dresser. I didn't even jump when the glass shattered. "You messed up too and I forgave you! I welcomed you back with no problems."

"Yeah and wanted me to be a fucking secret again. First it was hiding from your brother because you were scared of what he would say. Where was that fear when you went get married? Was your love for that nigga deeper than the fear you felt when it came to me? Had to be, because you didn't feel any fear when you said I do. That nigga had to mean more then and the fact that you want me to play boyfriend number two to that nigga, years later means he's more important now too. Go work on your marriage and I'll work on mine!" He said before ending the call. I went to call him back, but I kept getting the voicemail. Moments later, he blocked my number. I had no more tears left to cry, I was drained. There was nothing left for me to feel because just like that, I felt as low as I could be. Climbing into bed, I lay there until sleep found me. I felt wetness in my face and thought I was dreaming until I heard Malcolm's voice.

"Get up, bitch!" He roared. When I opened my eyes, I noticed the wetness was him pissing on me. I tried to block my face, but my body wouldn't cooperate.

"Malcolm, what are you doiiinnnggg?" I slurred obviously even more drunk than I thought I was. This nigga shook his dick off and shoved it back in his pants. I noticed he was drunk also from the way he saw swaying back and forth.

"All the fuck you did from the moment I married you was embarrass me! You are fat, ghetto and loud for no fucking reason. My parents told me you were trash, but I just had to do things my way. I tolerated your ass and you turn around and cheat on me!" He roared before punching me in my face. Now either I was numb from the liquor or he hit like a bitch. The shit didn't hurt at all.

"I- I never cheated. What are you talking about?" I asked, and he started fumbling in his pocket. When he pulled out his phone, he started scrolling before I heard my voice talking about how much I loved Corey and only Corey. I couldn't hear it all because her turned it off. "I was j-just confused. I never cheated though." I lied again.

"Stop fucking lying bitch! We saw you at the hotel!" He roared before grabbing me by the hair and dragging me out of the bed.

"AAHHHH! Let me go Malcolm. Baby, please let me go!" I cried out in pain. It was like he didn't hear me because Malcolm dragged me over the glass I broke and down the hallway as I kicked and screamed.

"Bitch, while you were cheating so was I and I saw you with that nigga! Don't fucking lie to me!" He said dragging me. Once we got in the front room, he threw me down and kicked me in the stomach with all his strength, the impact caused me to ball up into the fetal position and cry out. "How dare you cheat like you were the catch in this situation. You refused to have my kids, refused to be a real wife and refused to fuck me but you fucked that nigga!" He roared kicking me again and I screamed out. I prayed that someone heard me and as soon as I finished praying, the door swung open.

"What the fuck is going on?" Natasha asked running in.

"Natasha please help me. He- he is going cra-crazy!" I spoke through the pain I was feeling.

"Awww, poor poor Shailen!" She said kneeling down and rubbing my hair. "God forbid you get a broken heart. You don't deserve this, huh? Well neither did I when your brother broke mine! And you let him!" She roared standing up and kicking me in the face. I felt the blood start pouring from my nose and became dizzy. "I was your friend and you just let him take advantage of me!" She said kicking me again. This time she caught the corner of my eye. I didn't even realize I passed out until I was jolted awake by Malcolm dragging me by my hair to the door.

"St- stop." I tried to say aloud but it came out as a whisper.

"I want you out! Now! Natasha has been more than patient during this whole damn ordeal and its time I treated her like she should be treated. She's the type of woman my mother would love and be proud of." He said throwing me on the porch like I was trash. I lay there moaning as Natasha came out and threw out a robe, my purse, keys and cellphone at me before slamming the door behind me. Never have I ever felt so low. I 'm sure I had used my life's supply of tears just on this very day because I couldn't even cry at this moment. I just lay there numb to it all until I finally crawled to my car. Once I got there, I knew there was no way that I could drive in my condition, so I grabbed my phone and called Kewyn. I prayed that she was able to sneak away without my brother following. I really couldn't deal with anything more than I had already dealt with today.

15

K ewyn
　　Looking into Shay's face I couldn't help but to feel bad for her. This was proof of that saying, if you played with fire you got burned. The game she was playing was a dangerous one and she was on the losing end. At least, that first round because this was far from over.

"Stop looking at me like that." She said before walking into the bathroom. I went into the bags that I had just brought and pulled out some things for her to wear. "What's that for?" She asked, after she handled her business.

"This is for you. Get dressed so we can go." I responded as I ignored another one of Ty's calls. His ass really knew how to piss me off. Since last week when I left the damn park, he had been blowing me up. I asked too many times for him to stop calling and even went as far as blocking his number. His ass just called from a different one. As soon as Shay took the clothes back into the restroom, he called again and I answered.

"Why the fuck do you keep calling me Tyreek?" I angrily whispered.

"If you would stop blocking me and answer you would fucking

know!" He roared in the phone. "I could have been in all kinds of shit and your ass ignoring me for that black ass nigga!"

"Tyreek, you aren't my responsibility or concern anymore. I don't have to answer a motherfucking thing!" I quietly snapped back. "What the fuck is so important that you just keep on calling me?" I asked.

"Man, you only gave me ten stacks. Where the fuck I'm supposed to start over with that, salvation army?" He asked. Pulling the phone from my face I mugged the screen like he could see me. This nigga was acting like I gave him ten dollars.

"Bye Tyreek." I responded.

"Bitch hang up that phone and watch what happens to you!" He threatened.

"Nigga, if you even come near me Adonis will fuck you up." I said rolling my neck with each word. "Baby, he will not play behind me."

"Yeah?" Ty asked laughing. "Then who gone protect you from him? Huh?" He asked.

"No one needs to protect me from him? Adonis loves me, he would never put his hands on me." I said giggling at his dumb ass.

"Maybe not the Kewyn he thinks he knows. Shit but I'm sure you didn't tell him that all this shit was a game. Huh?" He taunted.

"So what. I lied about who you and Dez were but that's it! Everything else, was the truth. He loves me and I can tell him about that lil bitty ass lie." I shrugged.

"Use your head ma. That nigga deeper in the streets than anybody that you know. You know all street niggas got trust issues. You may tell him that shit and get away with the silent treatment for a few days. Then he may forgive you, true enough. But after I let that nigga know that me, you and Dez planned on robbing and killing him, then what? Bitch he going kill you! And I'll be long gone but its you that's going to be laid up with that nigga. Worse part is, you won't know when that other shoe going fall. That nigga can hear about this in the middle of the night and wake up and fuck you up." He laughed.

"Ty, wait..." I started. "What do you need from me? I can get a couple more thousand." I said.

"Nah, I want it all. Stay by your phone." He said hanging up in my face. The fuck did he mean by he wanted it all? What the fuck does it all include? I couldn't keep going in his safe and at the most I could withdraw a couple thousand from our account without too much concern, but that was it. I sat there thinking of how I could get more money until Shay came from the bathroom.

"Why are you all made up?" I asked. The hoe had even combed her green bundles into a high bun with her baby hairs laid.

"Well, my eye still hasn't healed, and I had to comb my hair up until I add another bundle. My shit hella thin from Malcolm dragging me by it last week." She said. Ty was far from my mind at this point and my mind was back on why I was here.

"Oh yeah, let's go." I said walking out the hotel room first. It was a lil later in the afternoon, but Shay still threw shades on her face. I know that she was self-conscious about the black eye but I would make her feel better in a bit. I pulled off into traffic and damn near flew to the house Malcolm and Shay once shared.

"Why are we here?" She asked as I pulled a cap on my head and pulled my bundles through the hole in the back.

"Shay, I love you like a sister. You asked me not to tell Adonis or Corrupt about this and I didn't. At this fucking point, you owe me. Bitch, don't act like you clueless as to what's going on. Get your house key and lets go in here and fuck some shit up." I stated going in my arm rest.

"What if Malcolm's home?" She asked.

"I pray he is!" I said pulling out my gun and cocking it. Me and Adonis went on dates at least four times a week. Our favorite date was the gun range, and I was real nice with my shot. "Let's go." I said climbing out the car. I waited for her to unlock the door and we walked in that bitch like we owned the shit. I led the way in looking from room to room but coming up empty. Entering the dining room, that bitch Natasha was laid out on the table with her legs in the air while Malcolm ate her like the Last Supper. The shit that blew my mind is he was ass naked with his booty tooted in the air. No real nigga left their ass in the air, ever. Shay looked pissed, but I was straight disgusted. I made sure my silencer was secured before I popped him in the ass cheek. Ignoring their screams, I looked at Shay. "Bitch, he used to eat your pussy like that?" I asked.

"Yeah." She said shrugging.

"And your pussy still got wet? I wish Adonis would." I laughed. "Get that bitch, Malcolm ain't moving no time soon." I said as Natasha cowered near Malcolm and his blown out asshole. He wouldn't shit right ever again. I had never shot anyone before, so I was shocked that I was so calm about this. After letting Shay beat Natasha's ass, we jumped her, and stomped Malcolm's ass then left. Since she was able to drive, she took her own car and followed me home. When we pulled up, I noticed a pretty ass Benz in the driveway. It wasn't better than mine, but it was nice.

"You know who that is?" I asked Shay.

"Nah, but bitch this looks like the car I been crying for. You know it's a bitch car from the color." She said, and I agreed.

"But why would a bitch's car that you don't know, be in my driveway?" I asked before walking away.

"You going the wrong way, huh?" Shay asked.

"Nope, gotta get my gun. I'm on a roll today!" I replied snatching it from my car and damn near running to the door. This nigga said he ain't have no secrets, he better pray to God that's the truth.

"You better not shoot my brother." Shay said laughing. I didn't even answer as I unlocked the door.

"Baby, who car?" I called out. I heard a bitch laughing and took off in the direction of the voice. When I saw who it was I calmed down for a second until I remembered Shay was with me.

"It's mine! Corey got it for my birthday!" Mika said smiling so big her eyes were closed. When Shay walked in, her smile fell. "Oh, and I got this too." Mika said wiggling her fingers. On her left ring finger set a rock so big the bitch was a boulder. The damn diamond almost made me drool. It looked like Cardi B's ring.

"Oh, that's nice." I dryly responded. Shit I didn't have beef with her but Shay was my girl so fuck Mika.

"Why do you have a gun?" Adonis asked.

"Cause I thought I was going to catch me a bitch slipping in my house." I laughed, but we both knew I was serious.

"You tripping. Later we going talk about how my gun made it to your car anyway." He said.

"You have so many, how do you know that this one is yours?" I asked.

"I notice everything. You took it this morning because yesterday, it was in its spot. I always check before I go to bed." He winked. "What's up Shay?" He asked his sister. Shay looked like she was about to explode.

"Nothing, I'm leaving." She responded looking at Corrupt. He didn't even gaze in her direction. I knew she was hurt because she had told me how everything played out between the two of them.

"Your brother asked you that." Mika said, I heard the attitude dripping in her voice.

"I know who asked me what." Shay spat back.

"You sure, because you were looking at my fiancé when you answered." Mika spat right back.

"Girl, fuck you and your tired ass nigga! How bout that." Shay said unable to control herself.

"If he tired, it's from the fat bitch he was fucking before realizing what he had. Gotta be a lot of hard work to lift your ass up and down." She spat, and my eyes bulged out of my damn head. I felt like Kevin Hart when he wasn't ready.

"What the fuck?" Adonis spat sitting up.

"That's right, your sister was fucking my man behind our back from the moment we came to town. Natasha told it all when I went to get my hair done." She said smirking like she did something. Corrupt looked like he was in shock.

"Oh baby, if you going tell it please tell it all and tell it right. What me and Corey had was before your time and that shit ain't ending cause we pissed off at the moment. This that love that goes on forever." Shay spat.

"Ring finger got his ring on it." Mika teased while wiggling her fingers again.

"Wrong bitch! Ring finger got my ring on it! See how you needed a guard on that bitch, that's cause it was sized for my fat ass finger, ask him! He gave that to you last night huh? For your birthday? I know because he gave it to me last night too. For your birthday. He asked me to marry him and I turned him down. But only after I nut all on that dick. Bet you paid him with head huh? How my pussy taste maw? And I'm not one hundred percent positive but if you got that car last night, I'm sure he had gotten it for me. I designed that shit and told him about it one day while he was eating my pussy like he was starving. Ask him for the paperwork, I'm sure it'll say my name cause he knows Shay ain't accepting shit in his! Ask him what that tattoo on his face says, in English. And when he does catch his head and come back, I'm accepting him with open legs bitch! So if you marry him, know that I ain't going stop fucking him! We sister wives bitch! Check mate, hoe!" Shay finished and stormed out. My damn mouth was hanging open.

"How the fuck could you embarrass me like that?" Mika cried to Corrupt.

"You did that to yourself ma. You could have talked to me about this shit at home." He waved her off.

"That's all you got to say? Fuck you Corey!" She screamed and ran out. On her way past me I tripped that bitch for my homie Shay.

"My bad about how you found this out bruh. Let me check on Mika and I'll explain tomorrow." Corrupt said walking to Adonis and holding out his hand. I knew shit was about to go left because he was quiet as hell through everything. Too quiet if you asked me. Before I could warn Corrupt, Adonis hit is ass with a blow so hard I jumped back. Corrupt fell to the ground, but quickly recovered and started swinging back. They went blow for blow but Corrupt was no match for Adonis and he must have known that because he pulled out a gun and pointed it at Adonis. I lifted mine and pointed it at him.

"Don't make do this Corrupt. You not shooting my man." I said with a shrug. I really didn't care about Corrupt enough not to shoot him.

"I don't want to shoot this nigga but he ain't about to beat me. I don't take l's ma. I know I'm in the wrong, so you got that. I violated but this shit deeper than a fuck between me and Shy. I love the fuck out that gah man! That's my fucking rib bruh." Did this nigga really say that like his fiancé wasn't Mika? Adonis didn't say anything as he stormed out of the dining room.

"You owe me a new table Corrupt." I said looking at the dining room table laying there destroyed.

"You got that. Tell Adonis hit my line when he ready to talk bruh." He said walking out and leaving the house. I followed behind him to lock the door when my text message tone went off.

000-777-9311: Help me rob that nigga.

Me: Who is this?

000-777-9311: Ty. With your help, I can get all the money I need and leave that nigga breathing. I'm only doing that cause I love you. You my first love and I'll do you that solid. But if you don't help, its lights out for that nigga.

Me: NO!

Me: There has got to be another way! I can get you more money. Let me make it to the bank.

000-777-9311: I said what I said. My team ready so set that shit up. I know he keeps a safe somewhere in that bitch. Not to mention the jewlery!

Me: I need time to think.

000-777-9311: We moving next Thursday with or without your help. If I'm doing it without your help, that nigga as good as dead.

I didn't even text Ty back as I fell onto the couch and silent tears rolled from my eyes. What the fuck was I supposed to do?

16

Adonis

Making my fourth lap around the block, I tried to wrap my brain around everything that was going on around me. A nigga had never been surrounded by snakes because I kept my circle small, only letting family in. What was I supposed to do when my family was the snakes? Shay ass knew to stay far away from me but Corrupt wasn't getting that message. For the past week his ass had been calling my line nonstop. At first I felt like he was being a bitch but then nigga texted me that he was a grown ass man and was only reaching out to put everything on the table. I could respect it. I knew I wasn't about to beef with my nigga or my sister forever but too much shit was happening at once. Even Kewyn's ass was acting sneaky. I watched her jump at her phone every time it rang. I had even watched her ass answer phone calls in other rooms in a whisper. Most rooms had camera's in them and if I wanted too, I could play that shit back. But I didn't need to. I was going let her tell me what was going on. Running up to my door, it swung open before I could touch it.

"Oh damn, you scared me." Kewyn jumped.

"Oh, for real? Where you going?" I asked in a dry tone.

"To the Mac store. I still can't find my laptop and I have some work to do on it." She said looking frustrated.

"Make sure you get the protection plan on it." I said.

"I'll just tell them hook me up with everything. You know I don't know anything about those damn apple products." She laughed and kissed me on the lips before leaving. Running upstairs, I took a quick shower before going in my office and locking the door. Opening the laptop, I went through the messages and caught up on what I missed. After I was done, I saved it then grabbed the ring that was in my desk drawer. I had sat down and designed this ring for Kewyn the day after we mad shit official. I had just gotten it the day Shay and Corrupt's shit came to light. No time since then seemed like the right time to propose. A nigga didn't need to be with Kewyn for years to know that I wanted to be with her for the rest of my years. I knew that shit before I slid in her.

"Hello?" I answered the phone for my mama.

"Well, you don't sound happy to hear from me." She said. "Have you talked to Shailen and Corey?" She asked.

"Nah, talk to them about what? I heard everything I needed to hear." I replied.

"Adonis, Shailen is your sister and Corey is your best friend. It's fucked up that they were sneaking around behind our back, but that shit is old. Let it go. Them dealing with each other recently, has nothing to do with us. They were grown!" She said.

"Ma man, Fuck all that! My sister is off limits to that nigga or any nigga that says he fucks with me!" I roared.

"Has Corey ever crossed you?" She asked.

"Nah bruh." I responded.

"Has he ever lied to you, stole from you, or have you ever heard of him beating up on bitches?" She asked.

"No, what you getting at though?" I asked hoping she would spit that shit out.

"Would you rather your baby sister end up with a man you've know all your life? You've trusted with your life? A man you've said yourself, protects her like you do? Or do you want her to end up with these niggas that's going beat on her, cheat on her and string her along?" She asked.

"I hear you bruh." I said before I heard the front door slam. "Let me hit you back, ma." I said ending the call and preparing to talk to Kewyn.

17

K ewyn
"Fuck! Fuck! Fuck!" I screamed punching the steering wheel of my car. I was so confused on what to do. I didn't want Adonis to look at me like I was a liar but I damn sure didn't want him to die. I thought I would be slick and just not give our address to Ty but he just bust my bubble. His sneaky ass knew where we lived, and I had led him here. After leaving the park, it didn't cross my mind to make sure I wasn't being followed home. Laying my head against the steering wheel I cried as I thought of what I had to go inside and do. I had to tell him and risk him no longer being in my life. Just the thought alone hurt my heart. I felt like I needed this man in my life and now I was damn near pushing him out. Walking into the house, I went to the room to save my new MacBook. When I didn't see Adonis in here, I knew he was locked in his office. He had never spent so much time locked in there before, but I knew that he was dealing with the Shay and Corrupt situation in his own way. Stripping out of my street clothes and throwing on some lounge wear, I went to his office and knocked.

"Come in." He called out. When I walked in, my heart broke. He was going through so much already and I was adding more to his already full plate. "Come see, Kewyn." He said sitting back in his chair. I walked over and got comfortable in his lap.

"What's wrong?" I asked him.

"Nothing. You got a nigga nervous about what you about to say." When he said that my heart skipped a beat. Did he know already?

"Say... Say about what?" I asked clearing my throat.

"I know that you have a past, we all do. I know that there are things you don't want me to know about your past, but I need to know. In order for us to move forward, I need to know that I know everything." He said pulling out a ring that I instantly fell in love with. "Before I give you this ring, do you have anything that I should know about?" He asked, staring me in the eyes. I felt the tears seconds before they fell down my face. It was already hard to tell this man what I had to say but now it was impossible. I had to find another way. "What's wrong Kewyn? You don't want to marry me?" He asked.

"Yeah. Yeah, I want to marry you!" I cried while wiping my tears.

"Why you crying then?" He asked.

"Because I'm so fucking happy that you asked." I lied.

"Ma, I need you to answer me. I love you so fucking much that a nigga can overlook damn near everything you were associated with in the past. Nothing or no one will harm you. In order for that to happen, you gotta open up. I want to marry you so fuckin bad. I want you to have my kids, man. I want to forever with you. I want to take you on vacations and fuck you on the sands of foreign beaches." As soon as he said that a light bulb went off in my head. "Do you have anything to tell me?" He asked.

"Yes, just that I love you so much and I accept!" I answered bouncing up and down in his lap. I had figured out a way to get Ty out of my hair and my man wouldn't have to know anything. Call me selfish all you want, I deserved his love. "Baby, why don't we leave and go on a vacation tomorrow. We can leave early in the morning and go anywhere but here!" I said.

"I'm cool with that. That's it?" He asked.

"What do you mean? Isn't that what you wanted me to say?" I

asked confused by his behavior. He didn't even look happy, but I simply assumed it was because of everything going on.

"I want you to say the truth. Whatever is your truth, I want to hear that." He said.

"Baby, I know the shit with Corrupt and Shay has your trust at an all time low, but this is me you're talking too. You can trust me with your life. I don't have anything in my past that would harm what we are building. I love you and I want to marry you!" I said. He nodded and placed the ring in my hand before kissing my forehead. I was taken aback because he didn't put it on my finger. I mean I wasn't engaged before but wasn't that how it went? I shrugged it off and slipped it on my own finger before kissing his lips.

"Rise up, I have to go holla at Corrupt real quick." I got up so that he could stand. "It's going to be late when I get back." He said and walked out. I wanted to say something about his attitude but maybe this was what he needed. Maybe he needed to get straight with his boy so that I could have the old Adonis back. Walking out of his office, I went to the bedroom and grabbed my phone. There was a missed call and a text. I ignored the call but read the message. I had saved the number under Shailen so that Adonis wouldn't answer if he ever saw it ringing. That's how bad their relationship was. Once I got Ty out of my hair, I would deal with their shit.

Shailen: Nine o'clock. Will you be ready?

Me: Change of plans, tomorrow night will be way better.

Shailen: Nah, I got a team ready now. It's going down tonight.

Me: Tomorrow you won't need a team. I'll leave the safe open for you.

When he didn't respond, I shrugged it off. I knew the deal was too good to pass up. Cracking open my new Macbook, I set it up until Adonis came home hours later.

"Hey baby, is everything good now?" I asked.

"Nah, shit all fucked up." He answered before going to the bathroom to shower again. I loved how clean he was. If he stepped foot out the house to check the mail, he would come back and shower. I climbed out the bed and went around checking the doors and setting the alarms. I was supposed to leave the back door unlocked while we slept and Ty would bust in like a robber, but thank God I was able to change those plans. Triple checking the alarm, I went back upstairs, and Adonis was already in the bed, so I joined him.

"I'm sorry that you have to deal with all of this bullshit bae. If there is anything I can do to make you feel better, let me know." I said.

"Thanks ma. Just keep it real with me about everything and we can make it through anything." He said. He seemed to be waiting on a response so I gave him one.

"I got you through whatever." He pulled me close and kissed me with a passion I had never felt. I loved each and every kiss he placed on my lips, but this one felt different. It felt like he was kissing me like he would never kiss me again. I know that's weird to say but, it just seemed like he was putting his all into this kiss. After a few moments he pulled me close and we fell asleep. Turning over in the bed, I heard the text tone on my phone go off and I quickly grabbed it so that Adonis wouldn't wake up but when I looked over, he wasn't in the bed anymore. Looking at my phone, we had laid down about two hours ago so where did he go. Clicking on the text, my heart dropped to my feet.

Shailen: We in, thanks for leaving the door unlocked. I know what I promised but ma, I can't let that nigga ride of with my girl. He gotta go!

Jumping out of the bed, I ran to the closet and grabbed a gun and checked the bullets. Before I could make it downstairs gunfire erupted from below.

"ADONIS!!!!!!" I screamed. "TYREEK NOOOOO!" My feet couldn't carry me fast enough. It was dark but with that the help of the moonlight I saw Adonis standing in the middle of the floor. As he and Corrupt laid niggas in mask out. They didn't notice the one creeping up behind them, but I did. Lifting my gun, I know I risked a chance at him being Tyreek but if I had to choose, he would lose every single time. The gleam of my gun caught his attention and he spun around and fired just as I did. My bullet hit him in the head and it amazed me how his shit exploded. When Corrupt and Adonis spun around their guns were on me. "It's me, it's me!" I called out with my hands raised.

"Awww fuck!" Corrupt roared looking my way. I couldn't read the look on Adonis' face. "She been hit!" I heard Corrupt say and I looked down. Blood was seeping through my gown, but I didn't feel anything and then I suddenly did. My body began burning and I saw Adonis run to me.

"Why did you come downstairs!" he roared with tears in his eye.

"I had... I had to save you! I rather me than you." I said before everything went black.

To Be Continued...

BOOKS BY TRENAE'

Sad to see the story end? Trenae' has a collection of other juicy stories for you to indulge in! Head on over to Amazon to one click or get them for free with Kindle Unlimited today!

The Sins of my Beretta 1

The Sins of my Beretta 2

You Gon' Pay Me with Tears 1

You Gon' Pay Me with Tears 2

The Sins of my Beretta 3

Wishing He Was My Savage 1

Wishing He Was My Savage 2

Wishing He Was My Savage 3

Dynastii & Tec (Standalone)

Wynter: An Ice-Cold Love 1

Wynter: An Ice-Cold Love 2 (3/24/18)

Promised to A Boss

Thick Thighs Save Lives (Anthology)

CPSIA information can be obtained
at www.ICGtesting.com
Printed in the USA
LVHW05s2323180618
581092LV00016B/1422/P

9 781986 838689